VOICES IN THE DARK

Lucy Devereux survives a car accident, but loses her sight. She also discovers she has inherited her grandfather's fortune. Then, to her horror and amazement, a young man comes forward claiming to be her husband. Lucy has no memory of him at all, but Doctor Harvey Sheridan thinks this could be due to her head injuries. Powerless to resist, Lucy is taken to live with her professed husband's family and soon finds herself a virtual prisoner. Convinced they are conniving to get her money, she appeals for help to Doctor Sheridan . . .

MAVIS THOMAS

VOICES IN THE DARK

Complete and Unabridged

LINFORD
Leicester

First published in Great Britain in 2005

First Linford Edition
published 2005

British Library CIP Data

20130816

Thomas, Mavis
    Voices in the dark.—Large print ed.—
Linford romance library
    1. Love stories
    2. Large type books
    I. Title
    823.9'14 [F]

    ISBN 1–84617–071–0

MORAY COUNCIL

DEPARTMENT OF TECHNICAL
& LEISURE SERVICES

F

Published by
F. A. Thorpe (Publishing)
Anstey, Leicestershire

Set by Words & Graphics Ltd.
Anstey, Leicestershire
Printed and bound in Great Britain by
T. J. International Ltd., Padstow, Cornwall

This book is printed on acid-free paper

1

'It's a beautiful day,' two or three people had said to me this morning and I knew that was right, because I could feel the sunshine warm on my face.

I could hear birds singing somewhere near, and the drowsy hum of insects in the flowerbeds at my feet. The flowers were a picture this year, people told me. I had to take their word for that.

'Such lovely roses,' mild little Miss Aylmer would murmur reverently each day when we took our strolls around these extensive gardens, her feathery hand holding mine to help my cautious steps. 'And the delphiniums are blue as the heavens, Lucy, dear!'

I was mostly called Lucy, seldom my more exotic Lucia. She could have called me anything. I was so deeply grateful for her friendship, even though the atmosphere of this place, the Hillside View Nursing/Convalescent Home deep in the Hampshire countryside, was always informal and cheerful — the whole aura due, of course, to the influence of the doctor in charge of us all, his dedication to our varying problems, his resolve to send us back into the wide world renewed in health and vigour.

His miracle had worked so many times, and it was working well with Miss Aylmer, despite her suffering such a bad fall in her eightieth year. The reason it hadn't yet worked with me was due to Dr Sheridan's extra difficulty in my case. Though I knew at once his reassuring voice, his steadying touch on my arm, I couldn't see him. I could see no-one and nothing in this peaceful haven where I had found myself.

Indeed, I had seen no glimmer of sky, no human face, since my last vision of daylight — the horrific instant when my grandfather's car skidded off a rain-soaked, forest road, to shatter among the huddled trees. He hadn't survived that terrible impact. I alone had struggled back to life, to a world of empty darkness.

Always, I would remember, somewhere far back through mists of shock and pain, two nurses negligently chatting by my hospital bed when they supposed I couldn't hear them.

'Do you know who she is? It was in the papers. She's the granddaughter of Senor Somebody, a big name in South American mines — silver, or was it copper? Anyway, she'll inherit whole pots of money from the old man! Not that it'll be much consolation now.'

'Well, one thing's for sure,' her colleague pointed out, 'if I had to lose my sight, I'd rather do it with money than without!'

At that time, I couldn't believe my grandfather was dead. Nor could I believe that when the bandages were taken from my face, I still would not see. Since then, belief had been thrust upon me, harshly and totally.

'Lucy, are you all right there?' a brisk, kind voice asked, jolting me back from those picture reveries my memory often painted on its darkened canvas.

I answered mechanically, 'I'm fine, thanks.' But then quickly I called the always so helpful Irish nurse back. 'Oh, Nurse Flynn, is it eleven yet? I'm expecting a visitor.'

I didn't say how shattering the visit would be. But she reassured me, 'Now don't you worry yourself! Dr Sheridan will see Mr Devereux first, and then bring him out to you. Everything's under control!'

She gave me an encouraging pat, but again I called her back.

'Nurse! Please, I just wish I knew, how do I look?'

'Now is it fancy compliments you're wanting, child?' she reproved.

Nurse Flynn never encouraged the smallest degree of self-pity. But today I really did need a truthful answer to my question.

Of course, even before the accident I

4

would hardly have been considered transcendingly beautiful. I was too slight and pale-faced for that, but then at least I had my glorious long hair to brush to a glossy tide around my shoulders. How much thinner was my face now, though mercifully, so they all said, unscarred? How different did the now slightly shorter hair make me look?

During these traumatic, muddled, groping weeks of learning to live in the dark, other things had mattered far more. But today, it was important.

'Lucy, you couldn't look unattractive if you tried!' Nurse Flynn touched my arm again as she went on her way. 'And it's almost eleven, so just take it easy now!'

Such simple advice. I wondered if Dr Sheridan had explained to her why this man called Devereux, a name completely unknown to me, was coming here to see me. Did she know he was claiming me as his lawfully wedded wife?

I couldn't believe it myself, not one

wildly-frightening word of the amazing story! But Dr Sheridan said it was quite possible, in a case like mine, that unfortunate lapses of memory and confusion would result from the head injuries I had suffered.

Out of the blue, Ralph Devereux had phoned Hillside View and explained that he had only just returned from abroad, and was appalled to hear about the accident and what had befallen me. He followed up the call with a letter to Dr Sheridan giving more details of the marriage, asking if it would be too upsetting for me if he came to visit. But still I had not even the smallest memory of him, of being with him or loving him as my husband. And how could that be, when I could recall quite clearly so much else?

I knew I was nineteen years old, and now quite alone in the world; that I had been orphaned as a small child, and cared for by a long line of nannies — financed by my grandfather from across the wide ocean, always too busy with his distant mines to give more personal care than sparse, brief visits. Holidays had been spent in his impersonal London flat, seldom used, with one of those paid guardians. Schooldays meant the discipline of a strict, almost Victorian boarding school.

It was only last year, I remembered clearly, that this cold life-pattern changed. Now nearing his eighties and becoming frailer, my grandfather had retired from the business world and come to settle in England. I left the school and went to live with him in the country home he had bought for the two of us, with its pretty, walled garden and sunny sitting-room. He allowed me to choose the furnishings and colours I liked. For the first time in my life I felt I was needed.

Very soon we became close, and I knew he much regretted it had come so late. The lonely old man, with his white hair and jet-bright eyes, became my world. He talked to me about his daughter, Esperanza, the mother I had scarcely known.

On many quiet evenings I played to him the piano he bought for me, finding we shared a love of music; he even insisted I had real talent and should study seriously. We discussed plans for holidays, because he wanted to show me the world I had never known.

Oh, I remembered so clearly all those plans we made! And as well, too vividly, that last evening drive through the beautiful New Forest near our home, that ended in stark tragedy. My grandfather suffered a fatal heart attack at the wheel. With no farewell, he left me alone in the world we had just begun to share.

★　★　★

'Just along here, Mr Devereux. Lucy is waiting for you.'

There were voices near and far in the sunny gardens, because, of course, I wasn't the only patient enjoying the summer air. This one voice I would never mistake, assured and authoritative but with warmth in it. This one voice that had comforted and steadied me from my first bewildering day here. Since then, it had become my eyes and my understanding, painting pictures that weren't just bare descriptions but cameo portraits of staff and patients and surroundings.

Harvey Sheridan was beside me now, asking quietly, 'Were you getting anxious? No, don't get up. Here's your visitor, right on time.'

His hand rested lightly on my shoulder. I knew he understood how I had dreaded this strangest of meetings, and so he wouldn't let me face it alone. He had tried to warn me that the first moments of reunion might not flood everything back, but I might remember something, the cadence of a voice, the fleeting picture of a face. From that, in time, the rest would follow.

The silence now after his quiet

greeting seemed interminable. I heard him at last prompt his companion, 'Well, speak to her. Let her know you're really here!'

'Lucy?' That was another voice, softer, shakier. 'It's Ralph. Do you — do you remember me now?'

It was the voice of a stranger. It meant nothing to me.

'Lucy? Surely you do know me?'

I shrank back from the touch of an unknown hand on mine. Catching hold of Dr Sheridan's arm I clung to him like a limpet. If this weren't strictly doctor/patient behaviour, I couldn't help it.

'Please,' I whispered, 'please tell me, what does he look like?'

His word images always conjured pictures, but not this time. A slimly-built man with curly light hair, brown-eyed, fair-browed. I couldn't form a face from that, perhaps because I was so desperately searching the spectrum of faces that had been part of my life.

'I'm sorry!' I blurted out. 'I don't remember! I don't remember at all!'

'Don't worry, it's no fault of yours,' Harvey reassured me. 'But it does present us with problems. Er — Mr Devereux, it won't help if you pass out on us, please sit down!' he added a shade sternly. 'Yes, that's better!'

I was no longer alone on the bench under the Hillside trees. This time I tried not to shrink away. It wasn't very successful.

'Well, I did warn you both not to be upset by a bad start,' Harvey said. He went on swiftly, not allowing this unnerving interview to linger in painful silence. 'I want to make things as straightforward as I can, and there's one thing we must sort out first of all. Lucy needs definite proof that her 'husband' is who he says he is before she trusts herself to him!'

He got no further. The man beside me broke in, 'Of course, my family told me I must bring some proof with me, especially because Lucy is an heiress.'

'Sensible of them,' Harvey said, a little dryly.

I realised there were papers being passed over. Harvey's arm freed itself from my clutching fingers as he took them.

'Hmm. Yes. A marriage certificate dated last December. Ralph Devereux and Lucia Esperanza Gray. This is a photocopy. You don't have the original?'

'Lucy had that.'

'I see. And this is a photo of you outside the registry office. Confetti, silver horse-shoes, the works. I can certainly recognise you, but —'

'My sister's husband, Matt, took the photos. I know it's not good of Lucy. The wind blew her hair all over her face. Her beautiful long hair . . .'

'So it would appear.'

'But wasn't it a pretty outfit for a winter wedding? That pale grey suit with fur trimmings.'

I choked suddenly. I was trembling,

the sense of unreality sweeping in anew.

'I do remember that outfit! Not anything else, but my grandfather bought me that suit not long before Christmas!'

'That's right, he did. Only you didn't call him Grandfather,' Ralph Devereux said softly. 'It was a little private joke. You called him Senor.'

'Yes!' I whispered. 'But how could you know that?'

'He liked sitting by the window, listening to the piano, smoking those strong cigars he wasn't supposed to have. And didn't you once threaten to throw a whole new box of them in your garden lily-pond?'

'Yes! Please, that's enough,' I stopped him, with a stirring of pain, raw and unhealed.

Cold, impersonal documents and a blemished photograph, they were one thing. But small, wholly intimate revelations like these proved that this unknown man indeed knew me well, and almost certainly I must be his wife.

I went on listening in numbed silence while the last yawning gaps were filled in, his soft, nervous voice describing my life as though it belonged to someone else. Evidently my poor grandfather was bitterly opposed to the marriage, forbidding me to throw myself away on Ralph Devereux. I learned how the old man's wishes were ignored. We ran away, secretly aided by Ralph's brother-in-law, Matt.

So it was a whirlwind elopement, a marriage to a semi-stranger, that had lain in the void of my memory! I marvelled that I could have inflicted such heartache on my grandfather. Had some great compulsion driven me, a magnetism in Ralph stronger than reason or duty? Was the face looking at me now a strikingly handsome one, that could melt away cold sanity?

But there was, it seemed, one real bond we shared, our love of music. We had first met in a Bournemouth concert hall, when we had to share a programme and I discovered Ralph knew of the music college where I hoped to begin. A haunting concerto, and afterwards a long walk by the sea under wintry stars, had been sufficient for us to fall in love. A storybook idyll all the way.

Only it was tragically short-lived, for just days after the over-hasty wedding we parted with tears and regrets. I returned to my angry grandfather, Ralph went on to complete a contract overseas, writing reviews around Europe for the Music International magazine.

The reason for the break-up was partly a simple clash of tempers between two people still almost strangers, and partly because I didn't want to go far away while my grandfather was so deeply upset.

At this point, Ralph stopped his monologue. Dr Sheridan prompted him.

'So you returned to your work and left your new bride to sort herself out as best she could?'

'Yes.' The low voice was scarcely

more than a whisper. 'She had to choose him or me. I know that was unforgivable.'

'It sounds like a pretty extreme reaction. So what happened?'

'She sent her ring back to me. She called herself Miss Gray again. Probably burned the original marriage papers, I wouldn't blame her! But I hoped it would blow over in time. She would make peace with the old man and maybe then he'd accept me. This is the reason I wasn't worried about not hearing from her for so long. And then just the other day I came across an old English newspaper. I read about the car smash.'

'It must have been a very bad shock. But why hadn't your family in England let you know? All the newspapers carried the story at the time.'

'Well, Matt was ill, And Molly, his wife, she's my sister, she doesn't read papers and she only looks at the soaps on the television.'

'I see. But — ' Harvey still evidently

wasn't satisfied. 'Surely Mr Alvarez's solicitors should have contacted you immediately.'

'They probably tried, but if they enquired through Music International they'd just draw a blank, because I lost the job.' Yet another fact in the sorry saga that he didn't attempt to hide. 'I didn't want Mr Alvarez to know that! So I was just killing time, drifting around, researching a book I might write. You can phone the solicitors for confirmation if you like! Gudge & Biksall. Shall I give you their number?'

The strange story made sense. It fitted together. If Ralph Devereux didn't emerge too creditably, the regret in his hesitant voice was clear.

Noticing the start I gave at the name of the law firm, Harvey asked, 'Does that ring a bell, Lucy?'

'Yes! I saw Mr Gudge when I went with Grandfather to their office in London, and he's in charge of the estate. He arranged for me to come here to Hillside. It's all paid for with an advance on my legacy.'

No-one answered that. Ralph just muttered, 'It was unforgivable to hide away just when Lucy needed me so badly.'

I had to say something to him, managing a strained voice that didn't sound like mine.

'No, don't blame yourself. You had no idea what was happening to me.'

They were virtually the first words I had spoken. So much of this reunion had been through a third party. Still I was trying desperately to realise I really had a husband to care for me and share the wreckage of my life.

'I know the past can't be altered,' his hesitant voice was going on, 'but if you're well enough to leave here I'll look after you.'

Harvey Sheridan interposed again.

'I already told you she could leave here providing she has proper care, certainly not otherwise!'

'Oh, I know how difficult everything will be. That's why I'm taking Lucy

18

home, somewhere she can feel she really belongs, with a family to care for her.' The stranger sounded deeply anxious. 'Lucy, we've engaged a resident nurse to look after you. And you'll have Molly and Matt to make you welcome, and their daughter, Davina, she's just eight, and she's longing to see her auntie and try to help. The house is down in Cornwall.'

If I had to leave the blessed security of Hillside, surely I couldn't hope for anything more than this? So often, through past lonely years, I had longed for the warmth of a family home, something I had never really known.

'It sounds very nice,' I managed to whisper.

He squeezed my hand gently. He had to leave very soon, he told me, a train to catch and arrangements to make. But first, we all went inside to Dr Sheridan's office, for coffee and ginger biscuits and more questions and answers. It struck me that I had seldom heard Harvey sound quite so brusque.

Most of all I was disturbed by the final part of the interview. He asked, 'Mr Devereux, you did suggest I contact Mr Alvarez's London solicitors to confirm your story, so you won't mind if I take you up on that?'

It was then, for the first time, impatience sounded in Ralph's voice.

'I thought we'd dealt with all that. Aren't you rather overstepping your responsibilities?' But then the anger subsided as fast as it had flared. 'No, I'm sorry. You're quite right. I should be grateful you're taking such care of Lucy. Here's the number. Ring them now.'

I wished Harvey would just say, 'All right, forget it,' because surely, if anything in Ralph's story were a fabrication, would he want it tested in this fashion? But Harvey did pick up his telephone, in front of us both.

He asked Mr Gudge's assistant outright, as my medical adviser aiding me with my affairs, whether it was known if, when, and where Ortiz Alvarez's granddaughter had been married.

Of course it was known. How could he have doubted it? It seemed every detail of the basic facts tallied with everything Ralph had said.

Harvey put down the phone with what sounded like a sigh.

'Well! That's that. If you two will excuse me, I've a day's work waiting.'

He didn't apologise for whatever lingering doubts had been troubling him. The door shut quietly behind him.

★ ★ ★

Sleep was almost impossible that night. My mind churned on and on as though it were a live presence within me.

The last moment with Ralph, when we were left alone, had been only brief. He said this must all be a great strain for me, and I needed to rest. He would return tomorrow with the nurse who would be caring for me, and we would all drive down to Cornwall. His farewell was very gentle, a brush of his lips against my cheek, an arm sliding around me.

But now this was a new day. Hillside View had awakened around me in its normal way, and Nurse Flynn was busy finishing my packing.

'He's a good-looking young fellow you'll be going away with,' she encouraged. 'I took a little peek at him yesterday.'

I answered her only with mumbles. And then somehow I was waiting on a sofa just inside the entrance, with my luggage around me. It seemed whole hours I sat there, clutching the white cane with which I had learned to steer myself around the house and garden.

'Well, well, and here's your car just coming up the drive! Oh, a big black expensive car!' That was Miss Aylmer who had been hovering anxiously around me, radiating the fragrance of her inevitable lavender water. 'Some real V.I.P. treatment you're getting, Lucy dear! I hope you'll be very, very happy, and you will keep in touch, let me know how you're getting on? I'll write you lots of nice, long, newsy letters, my dear. I'm sure your nice young man will read them to you!'

'I'm sure,' I whispered.

I clung to her hand. Though my eyes couldn't see her, they could still shed tears.

There were other good wishes and cordial, friendly hands, a whole round of farewells, and I scarcely recognised whose hands they were. But I knew Dr Sheridan was absent, and I knew I couldn't leave before he came.

'Lucy, have you been waiting long?' That was Ralph. 'I hope the journey won't tire you too much.'

Yesterday's voice was still strange in this world of strangers. The tears welled again, and I knew once they really started there would be no stopping them. My pile of belongings had been whisked away, and I doubted if I would ever find them again.

Someone else was enquiring, 'All ready, Mrs Devereux?' It was a girl's voice, crisply businesslike to the point of hardness. Its owner was introduced as Nurse Rita Greig, my companion-helper as long as I needed her. I wondered if she looked as she sounded and if at this eleventh hour I could flatly refuse to stir from the house.

Then came Harvey's voice, in the midst of growing panic.

'Just a moment. Don't rush her.'

This time, the silent tears fairly overflowed. I wept because I was frightened and lost. I wept because I was leaving Harvey Sheridan.

'Were they spiriting you away behind my back?' The familiar comfort of him swept over me. 'Come on, walk out with me. No need to hurry.'

There was so much I longed and needed to say to him. Thank you was so very cold, and goodbye was colder still. But before I found any words at all, he was telling me quietly, 'Don't let anyone rush you, Lucy. You've some big adjustments to make and all the time in the world to make them. Just do it at your own pace.'

Then he spoke over his shoulder. 'Mr Devereux, you'll be sure to book Lucy in at the rehabilitation centre I mentioned to you? That's very important. I used to work with Dr Farraday who's in charge there. I'll contact him in a while. Oh, and you did leave your full address in the office?'

'I told you yesterday, The Cliff House, near St Dawes Point, North Cornwall.'

'It sounds a little vague! I don't know the area, but I'm told it's a splendid coastline, well worth a visit.'

I was being helped into the back of a big car, seat-belted in, cocooned in cushions. Harvey hailed my new attendant.

'Nurse, I'd like just a few words with you.'

Their voices faded for a moment as they walked away. When they drew near again she was concluding with an officious, 'Certainly, Doctor Sheridan, you can rely on me.'

The doors were shut, and I was trapped. Still I hadn't said my farewell to Harvey, and now the wheels were moving, there was no more time. In just a few moments I felt already a world away from the place and the people that had been a blessed sanctuary.

It would be a long drive, but that didn't really matter much. After so broken a night, the motion of the car lulled me into a fitful sleep. There was soft music playing, and no-one spoke much. Ralph was sitting in front with whoever was at the wheel.

Nurse Greig, next to me, fidgeted a lot, asking me occasionally if I felt all right. A sickly spearmint aroma and vigorous chomping noises told me she was working her way through a pack of gum, unprofessional when escorting a patient! Nurse Flynn would never do that.

From a vivid nightmarish dream I woke suddenly to find myself alone with Ralph, while the others were inside a service station getting a meal. He asked me gently if I wanted to go in too, but I declined quitting my seat that was at least secure and enclosed.

'Why can't I remember you?' I blurted out in a sudden passion of frustration.

Ralph had an answer.

'Dr Sheridan said maybe it's because we quarrelled. Your mind blanked out something it didn't want to remember, trying to deny I ever existed, I'm afraid. But if we can be happy together, it might all come back to you.'

It made sense, Harvey's kind of sense. I basked in the thought, in the words, as though Harvey were beside me saying them to me. I slept a little more, and listened to the music, and endured more of Nurse Greig's busy jaws.

By the time I was beginning to feel I would never leave this car again, she gave me a poke in the ribs, her voice at its briskest.

'Come along, sleepy-head, time to wake up!' She spoke as one might to a small child as she helped me out of the

27

car. 'We're home!'

'Where's Ralph? I want to go with Ralph!'

'Oh, he's around somewhere.' Distinctly there was impatience in her voice. 'Straight inside to bed, those were the doctor's orders . . . whoops, mind these steps!'

As I stumbled up to this unknown abode, a new and effusive voice exclaimed, 'Lucy, my love, it's really you! Well, how wonderful! That young brother of mine has talked so much about you, I feel I know you already!'

Then came an unexpected brush of fluffy hair on my face, lips moist on my forehead. I tried not to retreat from Molly Wilson, but she chattered on regardless.

'Oh, you're shivering, you must be tired out. Let's get the poor child inside quickly, Nurse! I'll make you a nice warm drink, Lucy!'

I was becoming hypersensitive to the changes that passing through a doorway could bring. The fresh breeze on my face had gone, but the chief impression of this unseen house was a chill, echoing quality, creaking floorboards, a clock ticking heavily.

A man's voice was greeting me very cordially. 'How are you, my dear? So very nice to meet you again, Lucy!'

Again? But I must once have known Matthew Wilson, even if briefly, if he took those wedding pictures. Was there something in his voice I recognised? As he shook my hand, I wasn't sure.

This wasn't the last of the introductions, as there came next a child's sulky voice chanting obviously rehearsed words. 'Welcome home, Auntie Lucy, it's nice to have you here!' The title Davina used shook me anew. I couldn't grasp that not only had I acquired a husband, but also a clutch of unknown relatives.

Rita Greig took hold of my arm to order briskly, 'Come along, I'll take you upstairs.'

I found myself jerking away and

dissenting, 'No, I'll go with Ralph.'

That brought an impatient sigh from her, as I was passed over rather like a parcel.

Medleys of good-nights and promises of a nice little meal on a tray followed me up the staircase, carpeted stairs that twisted, then a landing. Ralph glided my hand along the wall and invited, 'There's the door. You open it.'

He left me a moment while he closed the window. I took a step and touched a chair with a cushion, beside a dressing-table that had drawers part-open and reeking of air-freshener. My questing fingers overturned a jar or an orna-ment, and as it rolled to the floor it carried something else along with it.

It had been a while since I felt moments of utter despair, but one came now. I cried out, 'It's no use. I'll never find my way about here!'

'Yes, you will. Of course you will. Give me your hand!'

Holding it, he walked me slowly, patiently, all around the room twice, three times. He put my hands on everything to feel and test. He described the dark-green curtains and bedcover, the buff carpet, the olive paint (a sombre apartment it must be!), an old bureau, a tiled fireplace.

His efforts were largely wasted, for I was unable to concentrate. When he left me for only an instant, I stumbled, and it was only his quick intervention that saved me falling.

It was then that I broke down completely. The tears of exhaustion and all the pent-up emotion of this endless day flooded out. I sobbed helplessly, scarcely aware of being lifted like a child and laid down on a chilly duvet.

He was smoothing damp hair off my forehead.

'It's been too much for you. Shall I call Nurse Greig to help you into bed?'

That was enough to start the tears flowing.

'Come on,' he said softly. 'When you've slept, tomorrow will feel better. And there's a nice piano downstairs waiting for you to try.'

Faintly my interest stirred. During these last weeks I had longed to touch a piano again. Did he really know me so well?

'Yes, it's the one I used to play. It was my most precious possession.' He stopped there as if sensing my unspoken question. 'That's right, used to play. You don't remember that story either? Oh, I was a real infant wonder, destined to go far, people said. I was still at school when I won a scholarship to the Lemarre Academy in Paris.'

I exclaimed, 'Did you really?'

'And to celebrate, my dad fixed up a family holiday. But the coach ran off a mountain road and rolled down. I lost both my parents that day. It was a mercy that Molly stayed with a friend instead of coming with us. I was badly injured but I recovered from all of it, except one thing.' Quietly, without bitterness, the serious voice went on. 'I never played another note. Take my left hand, Lucy. Hold it, don't be afraid.'

The slender hand could scarcely grip mine at all. I realised it was chilled and powerless.

'I — I had no idea,' I whispered. 'Oh, I'm so very sorry.'

'Since then I'm afraid I've never really got my life sorted out. My parents, the music, the whole future, it was like a wet sponge wiped out everything on a blackboard and left nothing. You know,' he confessed, 'I envy people like Matt, who know what they want and how to get it. I tried to get things together, teaching music, writing about music, but it didn't work out. It wasn't what I wanted. Oh, well!' He pulled up short there. 'This isn't the time for morbid tales. Can I leave you now and call Nurse Greig?'

He was still a stranger, a gentle-voiced ghost. But I found myself drawing his head down to me as I whispered awkwardly, very earnestly, 'I'm sorry I don't remember you. I'm truly sorry. But I promise I'll keep on trying.'

★ ★ ★

Emerging from the oblivion of heavy sleep, I heard footsteps approaching, and a hand fumbled at my door. As a laden tray bumped the wood, Rita Greig muttered an unprofessional, 'Oh, blast!' She followed it swiftly with a brisk greeting, 'Well, you're awake. Just in time for your breakfast. And it's another lovely morning, Mrs Devereux.'

She set down the tray and began busily plumping up pillows behind me.

'Try to eat all of it. Toast, scrambled egg — we've got to build up your strength. The sea didn't keep you awake long, did it?'

'The sea?'

'Can't you hear it now?' She pulled back a curtain and opened a window and then indeed I heard more than the laments of gulls. Somewhere close was a boisterous tide crashing and hissing against a cliff-face. Last night I hadn't realised it could all be so near. Last night I hadn't realised much at all.

'Please, can you tell me, are we far from the village?'

'St Dawes? Quite a way by road, even longer along the cliffs. This house was built here by some eccentric artist, so the story goes. It's just the place for the rest and quiet you need.'

I was glad she seemed to feel she had done enough, and left me with my tray. I sipped some coffee and set it aside and in doing so, overturned the beaker with the dregs of last night's drink, still uncleared from my table.

For a few minutes I huddled against the pillows. I couldn't eat. I wanted to get downstairs, but not with Nurse Greig's help. It would be too humiliating to have that patronising girl overseeing my every move. Tentatively I stepped out on to the carpet to search for some clothes.

With cloying fatigue and heavy sleep behind me, I could think again. And I thought of Harvey, far away in another world. I hadn't even said goodbye to him. He had seemed so anxious about my future, even unreasonably incredulous of Ralph's story. It seemed the obvious thing I must do would be to phone him right away, to let him know what was happening to me.

With this goal firmly in mind, I picked my way out to the stairs. From somewhere below, a raucous vacuum-cleaner vied with a blast of pop music. Then my heart leaped at a creak of the stairs under another foot than mine. I gasped. 'Who's that?'

Davina's voice, as startled as my own, answered, 'Only me! Can't you really see me?' Thoughtfully she added, 'You need one of those clever dogs that take people across roads, only Mummy Molly wouldn't let you keep it in your room!'

'Mummy Molly?'

'Oh, I call her that. She's not my real mummy. My real mummy died.'

'So did mine,' I said softly, and held

out a hand to her. 'Davina, you can help more than any clever dogs. Is there a telephone here?'

'Oh, yes! I'll show you,' she said importantly. 'It's just through — '

She didn't finish. The cleaner had stopped buzzing and her stepmother pounced on us.

'Davina, why didn't you call me like I told you? Now how did you sleep, Lucy? Where would you like to sit, my love?'

I had lost Davina's hand. It was Molly steering me downstairs. I asked directly, 'Please can I phone Dr Sheridan at the nursing home?'

'Oh.' She coughed, her voice all at once sharper. 'No, I really wouldn't do that.'

'Why not?'

'Well, even our Ralphie got the measure of him yesterday, and Nurse Greig has come across his sort before, haven't you, Rita? Doctors with bushels of charm and bedside manner, paying too much attention to their rich patients who're too poorly to see through it.'

'And he looked like a bad case,' Rita supplied acidly.

'You see, in your position you've got to be very careful, Lucy. It's a very good thing you have us to look after you!'

I felt as though I had been struck in the face. For once, with a spark of the Alvarez fire, I shouted at them both. 'You don't even know him, not anything about him. And I'm going to phone him now. I can if I like.'

'I'm afraid that won't be possible.' This time it was Matthew Wilson joining in. 'Our phone isn't working. It often gives us trouble out here.'

'All right! Does anyone have a mobile phone?'

'Yes, I have,' he assented smoothly. 'It needs charging up at present.'

I flared passionately. 'I don't believe you!'

'I hope you're not calling me a liar, Lucia'.

'Matt, don't be cross with her,' Molly

chimed in. 'It's no wonder the poor dear child is all upset and muddled, is it?'

'I'm not muddled,' I said clearly. 'If I can't phone, will someone please write a letter for me? Unless all your pens need charging up, too?'

No-one answered that, and I didn't pursue it. In a sudden nightmare of suspicion I wondered, would these people really write what I asked them to write, or send a letter to where I wished it to go?

It came to me with frightening clarity how helpless I was, cut off from the outside world in this isolated house, shut up here with these strangers who were merely voices in the dark. For a moment sheer panic surged in me, the beginnings of hysteria, until with huge relief I heard Ralph asking, 'What's wrong here? Lucy, what's the matter?'

Quickly his arm was around me. Yet another faceless ghost, but I had to trust someone.

'Ralph,' I whispered, 'will you take

me outside? Can we go for a little walk, just by ourselves?'

'That's right,' Matt agreed pleasantly, 'you take her for a nice stroll along the cliffs, Ralphie — the air will put some colour in her face. Only do take good care of her, won't you?'

Rita Greig cleared her throat officiously.

'Yes, don't let her go too near the edge. I think I should go with them, don't you, Mr Wilson? Just to make quite sure.'

2

The sea-birds screaming in the morning sky sounded very mournful. The ocean breeze took my breath away. I hadn't realised I would get tired so very quickly.

Though we weren't far from the house, I knew I was near the brink of majestic cliffs washed by a foaming tide. Never too near that edge, of course. True to her word, Rita Greig ensured that, her grip on my arm unrelaxing.

'No, leave it to me!' She had ousted Ralph from my side at the outset. 'I'll look after her. Isn't that what I'm here for?'

It occurred to me she was as ready to give sharp orders to him as to me. But he was clearly anxious about me.

Though I wouldn't admit to weariness, it was a relief when he finally insisted on a rest. While we sat together on a spread-out coat, he described for me a cloud-scudded blue sky, a grandeur of rocks and spray. No-one could bring a scene alive the way Harvey could, but I appreciated his trying.

The interlude didn't last long. Nurse Greig was soon pointing out, 'It's nearly lunch-time. We should start back.'

I had come out especially to talk in private to Ralph, but with Miss Greig around there had been no chance at all. I said gruffly, 'I'm not hungry and I like sitting here. Why don't you go on ahead, Nurse, and we'll follow when we're ready?'

'No, I don't think so. Unless you have proper meals at proper times, you won't get back your strength. Come along, ups-a-daisy!'

I couldn't stop her pulling me to my feet, not without the indignity of a struggle. But by now, anger was boiling in me. After all, I had inherited more than money and dark dramatic eyes

42

from my Grandfather Alvarez!

'Nurse, if you don't mind,' I burst out, 'I'd like to talk to my husband on our own — for once!'

As though soothing a petulant child she answered, 'Well, of course, dear. Don't get yourself excited.'

I bit my lip, annoyed still more at lapsing into what must look like a petty tantrum. She relinquished me immediately to Ralph, and I supposed withdrew from earshot because he asked me anxiously, 'Now, please try to tell me what's the matter.'

'Well . . . ' This wasn't what I meant to ask him, but I asked anyway. 'I don't like that bossy nurse. Why must I have her around? I don't need her, with you and your sister here!'

'Isn't that a bit unkind? It's all so strange to you here, shouldn't you give yourself time? Lots of time?' he said matter-of-factly.

Harvey had said precisely that.

'Lucy, this isn't like you,' Ralph pleaded. 'You know I promised Dr

Sheridan to have a nurse taking care of you. I can't go back on my word.'

In his own quiet way, he was good at placating my anger.

'I know that,' I admitted. 'But, if I explain it to him . . . ' This was exactly the chance I wanted, and I rushed on. 'Ralph, I do want to phone him. Please take me into the village this afternoon. Please?'

He coughed, as though wanting to delay an answer. But before he could reply, Nurse Greig was back.

'Sorry, the doctor gave me strict orders yesterday, no outings for several days. This little walk wouldn't count, but it rules out the village. Sorry!'

Had she listened to all our private conversation? There was no way I could know. Certainly she must have heard the last part, and Ralph hadn't warned me.

Suddenly all the fight went out of me. Wearily, I let them take me back to the house. What else was there to do?

There were aromas of Sunday lunch,

and it was served up soon after. Molly seemed distressed that I managed only a few mouthfuls. Rather than seating me at the table with the family she had given me my share on a tray in an easy-chair, solicitously cutting everything up for me, but it hadn't helped. I apologised, 'It's all very nice, but I just can't.'

'Don't worry about it,' her husband, Matt, reassured me. 'I'm sure Molly will fix you something special at teatime.'

Molly agreed at once. 'Of course I will!' But when she spoke again, her voice had changed rather disturbingly. 'Davina, you've spilled your orange juice again! You're the messiest, most careless child I've ever known, my poppet!'

Defiantly Davina retorted, 'I'm not your poppet! And I'm never going to be, either!'

Her father intervened sternly.

'That will do, Davina! Go up to your room, and don't come down till you can apologise properly to Mummy. You hear me?'

I sensed how the use of that word, Mummy, would wound the little girl, who had spoken to me this morning of her real mother. I heard her tempestuously leave the table, and the door bang shut.

'Take no notice,' Molly advised. 'We have our little problems. Well, all families do. Not that I haven't tried, but she's-oh, a difficult child.'

She dismissed the subject then with haste.

'Now would you like to lie down a while, nice and quietly up in your room?'

I didn't want to be banished as though I were as troublesome as poor Davina. Instead, I opted for a chintzy-feeling chair in what Molly called the side lounge, after Nurse Greig had marched me along a confusing passage. This rambling house was a labyrinth of twists and turns.

For maybe ten minutes I sat still. But

this morning's fatigue had passed, and I fidgeted in the lonely silence. The plaintive gulls outside were sad company. I wanted to find Davina, because we both needed the comfort of a friend.

Mostly by luck, exploring with my white stick, I found the door. Trying to recall how the passage turned when I was whisked along it, I nearly walked into a wall, and then almost upset a plant on a stand. It was the sound of voices, quarrelling voices, that made me stop short.

'Look here, Ralphie,' Molly's voice rose shrilly, 'are you a man or a mouse? All these years I've given you a roof over your head whenever you wanted it! Well, haven't I?'

'It's no use shouting, my dear, you'll only upset his artistic temperament. We don't want to suffer one of his melancholy moods.' Her husband's mostly level, cordial voice had a sharp edge to it now, an unpleasant barb of sarcasm.

'I . . . I didn't mean . . . ' Ralph's soft voice wavered.

'You never mean anything!' That was Molly again. 'You're too busy feeling sorry for your poor little self! You never make a decision in your life unless it's forced on you! Listen to me, just attend to your side of the business and let us attend to ours the way we're doing, all right? Can you get that into your head?'

I wished Ralph would shout back at the pair of them, but he didn't. Angry at his meekness, even more angry at them for speaking so harshly to him, I moved on so I wouldn't hear any more.

I made my way upstairs. On the landing I called quietly, 'Davina? It's Auntie.'

A door opened. She was crying, or she had been, still sniffing and snuffling as she declared belligerently, 'If they sent you to fetch me, I'm not coming down!'

'No-one sent me. I wanted to talk to you. Which is your room?'

She pulled me along the landing.

'You'll have to describe it,' I prompted gently. 'Can I sit down somewhere?'

'Oh, yes, here on the bed.' She perched on the edge beside me. 'They picked the horriblest room for me, I know they did! That big cupboard smells like cabbage, and there's mega-huge spiders in it. I'd like a room all pale-blue and silver, wouldn't you?'

I agreed, ignoring the truth of how little colour or pattern mattered to me any more.

'But you've some nice things of your own, surely? Books, dolls, games?'

'Well, I brought some books from our other house when we came here. Not dolls,' she said with scorn. 'And not games. There's no-one to play them with.'

'But you like reading?'

'Mmm. Mrs Harris said I was the best reader in the class, only Mummy Molly says reading too much is why I need these glasses. Ugly big ones, not frames with gold on like Megan at school has.'

49

I was building a picture of a lonely, somewhat plain little girl, made to feel plainer and unwanted.

'At my school,' I confided, 'I got in trouble for hiding in corners to read when I should have been doing other things. But I can't read your books now, of course.'

'I never thought of that. That's awful,' she said soberly.

'But you could read them to me, if you'd like to?'

She agreed eagerly, still sniffing but now diverted from her own woes. She started rummaging out stories I might like, chattering away without sulks or defiance, clearly delighted to have a sympathetic listener.

In the midst of it, a voice called from the stairs, 'Are you there, Mrs Devereux?'

As I jumped guiltily, Davina whispered with shattering disrespect, 'That's old Bossyboots Greig.' Both of us giggled until I shushed her in haste.

'In Davina's room, Nurse,' I called out demurely.

'Oh! I was looking all over for you, dear.' Miss Greig sounded quite concerned. 'Do let me know before you wander off, at least until you're used to the house. We don't want any accidents, do we?'

I replied even more demurely, 'I'm sorry.'

Was Ralph right, and I just hadn't given myself time to know her? Was it altogether too uncharitable to suspect her concern for my safety was rather less than her concern to hold on to a very comfortable job?

On her instructions I rested on my bed. I must have dozed, waking with a start when Molly arrived with a cup of tea. Dimly, I was aware I had been dreaming about Harvey, no formless voice but a real flesh-and-blood visible Harvey! A tall, strong-faced, dark-haired, kind-eyed man, he was waiting for me in the sunny garden at Hillside View among blossoming flowers and dancing butterflies, while I ran joyously along the path towards him.

It was hard to drag myself back to reality. A respectable, married woman really shouldn't revel in such dreams. The trouble was, of course, I didn't at all feel married.

'So he said to tell you goodbye,' Molly was rambling on. 'Aren't you awake yet? I'm saying, Matt didn't like to disturb you when he left. He has a bedsit, you see, near his work. He'll be back late Friday night. Not the best way to live, but his office begged him to stay on when we moved here. He's so valuable to them. He fits in all the hours he can.'

I wasn't really bothered about the merits or movements of Matt Wilson. His smooth cordiality seemed far less convincing after his unkindness to Ralph.

When I wriggled off the bed, feeling as rumpled and cross-grained as one does after a fully-clothed daytime sleep, Molly escorted me downstairs. A chair in the kitchen was of unwelcoming painted wood.

While she clattered plates and chopped salad, making me feel all the more useless, she chatted about her brother, who had slipped out for a walk. She told me how deeply he blamed himself for being absent at the time of the Alvarez tragedy. She also confided, in an all-girls-together manner, that Ralphie was crazy about me, head-over-heels in love ever since our first evening together in Bournemouth.

I voiced a thought that had puzzled me often.

'I can't understand why I was there without my grandfather. I never went out far without him.'

'Perhaps he just wasn't feeling well enough to go.'

'Then I wouldn't have gone either. I wouldn't have left him alone.'

'Oh, well, there must have been a reason at the time. Don't you worry your poor muddled head about it, my love.'

She moved on to other things, asking about the boarding school where I stayed so long, sympathising with my lonely life. When Davina came in the three of us shared quite a pleasant, quiet meal, as Nurse Greig was off duty and Ralph hadn't returned yet.

And yet, even through this interlude, my thoughts kept straying to Hillside View; those peaceful Sunday evenings with a church bell sounding nearby, gentle music in the big sitting-room . . . and Dr Sheridan, always, always finding time for a private word with me, and then the darkness was not quite so dark.

Presently, Molly left me in the lounge, with a radio for my companion offering a learned lecture on the climate of China, while she served the latecomers' meal. Sinking into a daze of depression, I heard Ralph's voice at last at the door.

'Lucy, I'm sorry I left you so long. I had to get some fresh air. How do you feel?'

I answered wearily, 'I'm fine.'

'But sick of sitting around? Do you

remember last night I told you about the piano? Would you like to try it now?'

Last night was a long way off. Now, I wasn't sure about making a fool of myself in front of the household. But Ralph was persuasive, steering me across a soft carpet to a music-stool. I put out an exploring hand.

'That's right,' he encouraged. 'The bane of Molly's existence, it's been gathering dust all these years.'

I touched two or three notes that sounded soft and clear. But still I wavered. 'It's kind of you, but, Ralph, I really can't do this.'

'Just try. With your two hands and my two eyes, we'll manage! Listen, I know you used to play this one.'

It was a fragment of Chopin, one of the simpler fragments that I had made my showpiece. Its familiarity rushed upon me now with an ache half pleasure, half pain.

'Come on, don't let me do all the work,' he insisted.

His fingers pressed mine on to the right keys, but the result was an uneven jumble until I found, uncannily, that my hands did know the notes they wanted, once so diligently mastered. It was a stumbling, fumbling performance, but the realisation that there was one door still not immovably closed filled me with an elation of triumph.

'I did it! Ralph, I did it!'

'You did! Shall we try again?'

We did try, that and other pieces I used to know, his one hand producing more music than my two, patiently filling in these strange three-part duets. For this little while, as my confidence grew, I lost track of the time that dragged so tediously. The enchantment of music I loved, of concentrating and achieving, and perhaps as well the understanding presence at my side, brought me nearer happiness than I could have dreamed possible.

I could have stayed at the piano far into the night. But all too soon a tap on the door heralded Nurse Greig.

'Excuse me. It's nine o'clock.'

'Oh, I'm not ready for bed yet,' I exclaimed. 'We're getting on so nicely!'

'So I heard. But you need your rest. Those were my orders.'

My ready irritation with her flared anew. I still had a mind of my own.

'I'm not a child, and I'll go to bed when I'm ready! Ralph, can we try the Brahms' Lullaby again?'

He could surely have supported me? But, no, it seemed liked a repeat performance of our stroll out on the cliffs. Nurse Greig addressed him directly, 'Mr Devereux, I'm doing my best for your wife, so will you please say good-night to her?'

He muttered unhappily, 'Lucy, she does know best. Please don't get upset.' The appeal in his voice was unmistakable, and for his sake alone I gave in.

He whispered a wish that I should sleep well, and then he held me and kissed me. It was almost a child's kiss, just brushing my cheek. But as he started to move away, some instinct made me cling to him, his unseen face warm against mine. Partly it was pity for his own troubles, partly a very real gratitude, and as well the dawning realisation that maybe the sole salvation for us both must be in my learning to love him again. Would it be such a hard task?

Neither of us spoke. I realised he was gently releasing my hold, as there came a half-suppressed grunt of impatience from Rita Greig.

If it annoyed her to wait on the sidelines while our basic good-night became a little more, that was too bad. It really was none of her business!

★ ★ ★

That night, as on so many, sleep was elusive. In some strange way, as the evening's elation faded and reaction set in, I realised there was no going back from this new world, no laying it aside to be continued when I chose. This dimly imagined house of strangers, with all its uneasy undercurrents, was really my home. I had no other, except maybe the house I had shared so briefly with my poor grandfather, and that I knew was already on the market. It was the main decision I made after the accident, never wishing to set foot in it again.

When finally I awoke from a doze, heavy-headed, Nurse Greig was drawing back the curtains. Today there was no slipping away downstairs. She hustled me along the landing for a shivery bath, and then I was placed at the table below to breakfast in solitary state.

It was a dreary start to a long and tedious day. Molly bustled around with her vacuum cleaner and loud transistor, before departing by car for the village shops, taking Davina with her. Ralph was busy in the garden. When Nurse Greig began reading aloud to me from a magazine in a bored and boring voice, my thoughts drifted off, as ever, to Hillside View.

Where was the nice, long, newsy letter Miss Aylmer had several times promised to send as soon as I arrived here? And had Dr Sheridan forgotten me so soon, or had he maybe tried to ring and been defeated by the faulty telephone?

Another session later at the piano was disappointingly unlike last night's, because Nurse Greig stationed herself, and her habitual gum-chewing, in the room to enjoy the music. Molly came in as well, with a tray of coffee. During a pause she switched on a tape-recording somewhere nearby, asking, 'Here, Lucy, you're a connoisseur. What do you think of this?'

Momentarily I was enthralled by a most sensitive and dramatic interpretation of part of the Beethoven Pathetique Sonata, until Ralph muttered something and left the room. A lightning intuition made me exclaim, 'I know what this is!'

'Yes, Ralphie recorded it a few days before his hand was hurt,' Molly confirmed. 'He was, oh, sixteen years old. Eight years ago! Not my sort of music, but wasn't he pretty good?'

'Pretty good?' I echoed. 'That isn't training or winning fancy prizes, that's something much more.' Then anger took hold of me. 'But it's cruel to play it in front of him!'

'Lucy, you mustn't think that. You see, it's best for him to face realities. I've tried all I can to help him. At one time he wouldn't even look at the piano, let alone play like he does with you. Sometimes I've had to really nag him, or he'd just have wasted away with regrets.'

Subdued, I muttered, 'Oh!' I was recalling my accidental eavesdropping yesterday, the heated family scene that perhaps I misunderstood. Was it true that Ralph sometimes needed to be bullied for his own good?

For a moment I sat quietly listening to the music until Molly switched off the player. Then I asked her rather shakily, 'Can't anything more be done for his hand?'

'We went to specialists, of course, but

they said it's hopeless. Oh, there's one chance left, but it's very remote. You've probably not heard of this special clinic in California.'

Nurse Greig intervened crisply, 'You mean the Anstey Vance Clinic? They use a revolutionary new treatment, deep massage allied to bone-grafts, I believe. Still in the experimental stage.'

'Oh, dear, Nurse, now you're smothering us with science! But, yes, that's the place, and Matt did make enquiries but well, apart from the huge cost, we weren't sure it was wise to build up Ralphie's hopes.'

I reflected privately, whatever the cost of weeks or months in California, my inheritance would be better spent helping Ralph than sitting around in bank accounts and investments. But the situation wasn't that simple. And there was just one person ideally qualified to advise us, whose medical knowledge matched his human understanding.

Excitedly I exclaimed, 'I'll ask Dr Sheridan, I know he'd help us.'

Rita Greig killed my eagerness stone dead.

'I can tell you for sure, he won't give any opinion on someone who isn't his own patient. Ethics, Mrs Devereux.'

'That's quite right,' Molly agreed anxiously. 'No, Lucy, it's best to forget about the Vance place. Now how about some more coffee?'

I accepted it, too weary to refuse. But I wouldn't forget the Vance place. It was some sort of goal, something I might achieve, for Ralph who had been so kind to me.

And the thought remained clear in my mind through the long hours that followed, despite all my growing frustrations and doubts about my position here at Cliff House. Already I had decided that whoever designed this isolated dwelling, many decades ago, certainly took no account of a sightless inhabitant in after years. It seemed the most confusing, unwelcoming pile of bricks and mortar imaginable for my affliction. But I resolved from the start never to seek help unless it was absolutely vital, except maybe from Ralph or Davina. I would avoid Molly's over-zealous smothering and Nurse Greig's brisk marshalling at all costs.

That was why, on Tuesday morning when I found during my solitary breakfast that I needed a cardigan from my bedroom, I sought no aid. Rita Greig was in the kitchen with Molly. Ralph was in the garden, Davina had melted away; it seemed almost as though both were avoiding being alone with me.

Well, I could look after myself. I found my way upstairs, along the landing to where the door of my room should be. I had found it several times before. Only this time, this infuriating house was up to its tricks again, so when I opened a door I suddenly doubted if this were indeed my room. A tinge of perfume told me it could be Rita's or Molly's. If I caught a whiff of spearmint, I would know for sure.

Then I tripped over something,

probably a discarded slipper, and clutched at space, and fell to my knees on the carpet. Most of all, I didn't want the room's owner to find me blundering about there. I scrambled up and retreated to the door, except the door wasn't there.

I stumbled into a rumpled bed, then a stool. My questing hands were becoming frantic. The door must be somewhere among this confusion of walls and furniture! Then at last there was a door, but when I opened it my probing hand plunged only into clothes hanging in a cupboard.

I backed away, my heart drumming in the aching darkness, until eventually my wild heartbeats stopped as I froze with sheer terror.

My outstretched hand had touched a head . . . dear heaven, a head? Cold, faceless, covered with long hair that entwined my fingers. I let out a sound that was scarcely a scream. As I fell to the floor half-fainting, I was just aware that the disembodied head was falling with me, the hair coming loose in my hands, smothering me with its sickening softness.

It was a child's voice, far across the mists of the nightmare, that pulled me back to reality. Davina's hands were touching me, her anxious breath was on my cheek.

'Auntie! Are you all right? You've knocked down all Nurse Greig's things. She'll go spare if she finds out! Her wig is all tangled up . . .'

I whispered, 'A wig? Is that what it is?'

The wig-stand and long-haired wig, which I has pulled down as I fell, still lay harmlessly beside me. I didn't care now that they had almost sent me into hysterics. I was only human, and robbed of the safety of sight.

'You made such a funny noise,' Davina was going on. 'Are you ill? Shall I call someone?'

'No, don't! I'm all right now.'

It wasn't true, for I was still utterly shocked. I held on tightly to the child for a moment, the warmth of her body comforting me. She said darkly, 'She won't like you being in her room. She was cross when I came in here.'

'I got lost, it was just an accident. And I was scared when the wig fell down.' My thoughts now were racing wildly. 'Davina, what colour is it?'

'What colour? Black, same as your hair! Except yours is shorter. This is really long.'

As long as mine once used to be? As it was in the winter when I became Ralph's bride, its flowing strands blowing across my face in the wind to spoil our wedding photographs . . .

'I bet old bossy Greig looks a sight when she wears it!' Davina produced some rare giggles.

I let her help me up, and sat on the edge of the bed while she obligingly straightened the room. It took only that short space of time to reach a huge decision.

'You've been such a help, and I wonder if you could help some more. I have to go to the village. It's really important.' I skirted around my quite desperate need to reach a telephone. 'Everyone thinks I'm not well enough, so they won't take me. But I'll go by myself, if you'll just tell me how to find the bus route.'

'You couldn't!' she exclaimed, obviously aghast at that rash idea. 'You wouldn't ever get there. It's miles!'

'I have to try. It really is very important.'

'Oh, well.' She hesitated, sniffing, pondering. 'I know the way. I'll take you there if you like. Don't worry, I can look after you.'

The offer was understandably a little patronising but I was deeply grateful; and also alarmed at what I was doing, because Davina's mixed-up little life had enough problems. It was wrong to involve her in this scheme, to incite disobedience to her parents. But just now, my half-formed fears and my fever of longing were beyond all resisting.

We escaped safely from Miss Greig's room, and soon after lunch was on the table, as usual masquerading as a happy, chatty, family meal. I tried to eat, to avoid causing trouble. Then I pleaded a headache and retired to my room. The household, or most of it, wouldn't miss me.

At the last moment I had wanted to pour out my tale to Ralph, to beg his help, but I had no chance. Was he really avoiding me deliberately, ever since our moments of closeness on that evening at the piano? Was it just my imagination?

This was all part of the confusion I must describe urgently to Harvey Sheridan, and he would know the answers, would know what to do! I had to speak to him, whatever the risks, whatever the trouble it caused. I had to hear his voice again.

It wasn't long before my door was cautiously opened and Davina whispered, 'Are you ready, Auntie?' I was ready. She found my coat and bag, clutching my hand as we crept down the stairs.

She opened the front door, and almost bundled me headlong down the steps and along to the gate.

Soon I was panting for breath, every nerve straining not to trip and fall, clinging to the child with a grip that would pull her down as well if I stumbled over.

I had never thought the world would be so vast, on this first taste of it without proper supervision. My own helplessness shattered me.

Davina screeched, 'A bus!'

It was someone other than Davina who steered me to a seat on the bus. A kindly, motherly, London-accented voice, already in charge of several rioting children, included Davina and me with the rest of her brood.

I was almost sorry when the vehicle pulled up in St Dawes and I had to move again. The helpful mother was alighting, too, and instructed briskly, 'Come on, duck, you hang on to me.'

She insisted I needed something hot in my stomach, and ferried me to a café. Soon we went into warm air scented with cooking and coffee, and the chink of china.

She left us only after ensuring we were supplied with hot soup and home-baked rolls. I never found out her name. I never had a chance to thank her.

For a moment I gloried in comfort, warmth, reviving strength, until it dawned on me I was frittering away precious time. I was here in the village, within reach of a telephone.

'Davina, would you look in my bag? There's money for the bill, and I'll need some for a phone call . . . Please,' I hailed the café proprietor, who sounded an elderly, kindly soul and was hovering nearby, 'I must phone someone, it's terribly important. Is there a call-box somewhere?'

'Down by the post office. Across the road, my dear. But you could use my phone if you like.'

I accepted gladly. Davina was tugging at my arm and whispering that she could find no money except a few pence, but that could be sorted out in a moment. I knew I had brought a good sum in ready cash away with me from Hillside. Somewhere at the back of the little tea-shop I was settled on a stool, clutching the telephone with a suddenly shaky hand. At last a helpful operator was saying, 'Go ahead, caller!'

'Hillside View, can I help you?' That was Miss Carstairs in her administrative office. A great wave of something akin to homesickness broke over me.

'It's Lucia Gray!' I blurted out.

Not for one moment did I think to say Lucy Devereux.

'Oh, yes, Miss Gray. How are you getting on?'

'Thank you, I'm all right.' I could hardly get the words out. 'Please, can I speak to Dr Sheridan?'

Why was the woman hesitating so long? And then her words were like a blow in my face.

'I'm sorry, Dr Sheridan is engaged with a new patient. He gave orders not to be disturbed. Can I take a message?'

I bit my lip, unable to answer. I heard her ask twice for my number, verging on impatience now. And then came a pause while she seemed to talk to someone nearby.

Then she came back to me.

'Miss Gray? The doctor just looked in to check a file. I've told him you're waiting and he'll speak to you. Will you hold while he goes to his office?'

For a small eternity I waited, until another voice spoke, that voice so often remembered, kind, warm, concerned, reassuring.

'Lucy? Is that you?'

3

'It's very nice to hear from you,' Harvey said. 'How are you settling in down there in Cornwall?'

'I'm not settling down! Not at all.' Now this longed-for moment had come, I could only stutter and stammer. 'I don't like it here. I've been so worried and frightened! Oh, I've had such an awful time! — '

Then, all at once, nothing could keep the words back, showering him with facts and fancies — the isolated house, the strangers whose outward pleasantness barely concealed disquieting family conflicts; but most of all, how I was constantly shut in, closely watched, barred from telephone calls — and how could I know if they would pass on any correspondence, private or business? And all the time, my questions were met by their monotonous mantra, don't worry your poor muddled head.

'I'm not imagining it,' I insisted. 'Oh, you must think it sounds very silly!'

'Not silly, maybe a little bit out of perspective? It's only natural that you're obsessed with your own thoughts and feelings, but have you considered it from their viewpoint? Couldn't they be trying so hard to protect you that they're just overdoing it all?'

I mumbled a deeply disappointed, 'Um.' I hadn't made him understand.

'Wouldn't it help to discuss it with the nurse who's looking after you?'

'No, I wouldn't discuss anything with her, even if she did train at St Paul's Hospital or wherever!'

'She did. I checked on that. Come on, let's have the unvarnished facts. Has she ever been unkind to you?'

'I suppose not. But I can't make friends with her.'

Even to my own ears, my unvarnished facts sounded very childish. I went on, 'I did ask Ralph to dismiss her, but he won't. And she gives him orders almost as much as she does me.'

I didn't pursue that side of things. I still had to recount my horrific encounter with the long-haired wig. Hysteria still wasn't gone from my voice when I described it.

'Long black hair, like the wedding photo Ralph showed you, do you remember?'

'I remember. But why especially like that?'

'I don't know!' I said quite wildly. 'But I keep thinking, I hadn't worn my hair loose and floppy like that since I was Davina's age. And I'd have wanted it tidy that day, wouldn't I?'

'Perhaps Ralph specially liked it that way. Haven't you asked him?'

I confessed that I hadn't. I couldn't say any more. Harvey had an answer for everything, as I had known he would, but they were the wrong answers. And his next words were the very obvious question, 'Where are you ringing from now?'

'Oh, a café in the village, St Dawes.'

Which sounded as though I wasn't confined to the house at all.

'Well,' he was saying, 'I'm sorry to hear you've had a bad start. I hope you'll soon settle down much better. I'll try to contact you sometime, but if you'll excuse me just now, Lucy, I'm keeping someone waiting.'

I wanted to cry, and the unshed tears ached and burned. It would have been better if I hadn't spoken to him. I said, 'Goodbye!' short and sharp.

Only vaguely, I was aware of sounds around me, chinking tea-cups, murmuring voices. I had drifted briefly into another world, and that world had rejected me. As I moved forward, my hand touched a table, a chair, another chair. Then I was in the strong draught of the open door as someone just entering the café brushed past and held the door for me. I felt cool air, falling rain, a vastness of unreality.

It seemed someone was calling out, but I wasn't sure. I jolted down a kerb and all around suddenly became an

ominous rush of sound, a hiss, a scream
. . . tyres on a rainy street, the searing
shriek of brakes. As I fell, I felt no
physical pain, only my face against the
wet roadway. Still the unshed tears
ached, and still I couldn't cry.

Though I didn't lose consciousness,
everything had become a far-off haze of
voices and ministering hands. And then
I realised the hands were folding a
blanket round me, pillowing my head
on a cushion. It wasn't a bed, but some
sort of sofa. A child was sobbing close
by.

Probably it was the café owner who
was explaining I had slipped off the
pavement right in front of a car. The
driver had just managed to stop, and I
had escaped injury, but I was badly
shocked and needed medical care.

Davina sobbed even more at the
idea of ambulances and hospitals. I
mumbled, 'I just want to go home.
There's a nurse there.'

'All right, my dear,' the voice
soothed. 'If you'll tell me your name

and where to call them, so they can fetch you?'

Davina came up with all the details. I was too exhausted to do more than lie still while they sought help. I was shivering, my head ached dismally. Perhaps my heart ached even more. For a timeless interlude I waited there, until more people were talking near at hand, not the café people. One voice meant always kindness, and at this moment I needed that badly.

I whispered, 'Ralph?'

He asked no questions, he gave me no reproaches, he just held me. I tried to say, 'Take me home. Please, take me home.'

'You're going home now, Mrs Devereux.' That was Rita Greig, but I was even pleased to have her here.

Rolled in my blanket, I was lifted like a child. I clung on to Ralph weakly. In a moment I was in the back seat of a car, still held in his comforting arms, with Davina snuggling up beside us.

Soon I lay in a sort of weary bliss in

the comfort of my own bed, but even that wasn't enough to stop me shivering.

'I'm here.' Ralph's hand held mine fast. 'Just try to rest.'

Drowsily I thought that he didn't deserve to be here among people who appreciated neither his gentle kindness nor the fact that his musical gift was ruined.

I whispered, 'I'm sorry, I'm so sorry for being such a trouble.'

'Please, don't say that. Just promise you won't do such a thing again. If anything happened to you . . . ' He trailed off, his voice breaking.

I hadn't been sure how much he really cared for me, but I knew now. As he bent to kiss me, I knew. It was no childlike kiss this time, but his lips warm and searching full on mine, a man's loving kiss for a woman, sweet and strong, just a little frightening.

One kiss, only one. He stroked my hair, and tenderly touched my face . . .

There was just one time during that

long night that I awoke. Or at least, I thought I was awake, but it must really have been a dream. I was aware of a strange, blurred glimmer of a lamp across the room, an unfamiliar room filled with dark shapes of furniture. There was a girl's slim figure leaning over the bed, adjusting the covers. I could even see her sharp-featured face in profile.

'I keep on telling you,' she was whispering impatiently to someone else across the room. 'She's not hurt, she'll be fine. No need to keep fussing!'

'I still think she needs a doctor.' I recognised Ralph's voice, and I strained to make out the shadowy form at the foot of the bed. I knew only that a man stood there, slightly built, his hair light-coloured, his face turned away from me.

'Look, will you believe me?' Rita Greig hissed at him. 'For heaven's sake, Ralphie, are you the qualified nurse, or am I?'

It was when I heard her use the

family pet-name 'Ralphie' that I knew it was indeed just a dream.

★ ★ ★

My chief legacy of that eventful day was a severe chill. I spent the next couple of days in bed, and on the next ventured only as far as the sitting-room.

Several times Davina smuggled herself in to be with me. Nurse Greig read aloud in her bored tones, Molly showered me with chocolates and sympathy. Ralph, most comfort of all, brought his tape-player to share mutually favourite music.

I was more and more concerned that I hadn't heard from the solicitors arranging Senor Alvarez' affairs, not even an acknowledgement of my new address, which I knew Harvey had personally given them. I kept remembering how Miss Aylmer at Hillside had promised she would write right away, but where was her letter? And Harvey hadn't been in contact, though I shouldn't think of Harvey.

Late on Friday evening, after I was settled for the night, I heard Matthew Wilson come in. I thought, too, I heard sounds of an argument downstairs. After another restless night, I was astir well before my breakfast tray arrived the next morning, because a most startling thought had flashed into my mind.

On the day I so nearly became a road accident statistic in St Dawes, when an SOS for help brought Rita and Ralph rushing to collect me, *how* was that message phoned to a house that didn't possess a working telephone?

Matt Wilson greeted me at the breakfast table downstairs.

'Well, my dear, how are you? Much better, I hope?'

'I got soaked in the rain. My own fault,' I said flatly.

'Well, I have to drive into Camborne on business. I'll take that scamp, Davina, so she won't get under your feet. It's a lovely morning, and when I get back I'll expect a nice sun tan on that peaky face. Ralphie, make yourself useful, a deck-chair for the lady!'

It seemed to me Ralph was very quiet and subdued today, even more than usual. I let him take me outside, because this was just the chance I wanted. I waited till we were alone in the sunny garden and all was quiet.

'Ralph, will you tell me something? The other day, in the village, when they phoned from the café for you to fetch me . . . ' Somehow I kept the words coming. 'I don't understand how they did that if the phone here doesn't work.'

It wasn't his voice that answered. I leaped in my chair with shock and anger, as Rita said right at my elbow, 'Excuse me, I can tell you the answer.'

I blazed at her, 'Don't creep up on me like that! You're always doing it!'

'I was just bringing you a drink,' she said sulkily. 'I couldn't help overhearing. It's true the telephone in the house is faulty. Mrs Begg at the café couldn't get through, but we were already out searching for you in the car. St Dawes was the obvious place, and we soon found someone who'd seen the accident. It's quite simple, nothing to get upset about.'

Still unconvinced, I sighed wearily. There seemed nothing else to say.

Presently, when the noon warmth was drowsy in the garden and Ralph left me for a while, I was still resting with my feet up and my head back. But I was tired of resting. Tired of sitting still, tired of puzzling and supposing.

'Lucy, are you awake?' That was Ralph back again. 'Can I speak to you while we're alone?'

Really alone, I thought bitterly, or was Nurse Greig there?

'It's about us,' he began hesitantly. 'We're living here like friends or brother and sister. But we're not brother and sister, are we?'

'I know.' I felt colour flood my face. 'You've been very patient. But, Ralph, I just don't feel . . . '

He said the words I couldn't bring myself to utter.

'You can't remember any wedding. You can't remember us being together. I do understand that, but how long can we go on living this way?'

'I know,' I whispered again. I had no solution to offer.

But he had one.

'There's a way out. Suppose we get married again?'

I struggled to think clearly, and I couldn't think at all. It sounded so sensible, so simple. A second ceremony to confirm the first that was lost in the mists of my confusion, a renewal of vows I couldn't recall taking.

The word he sought quivered on my lips. But then there came a shout across the garden, and the word was still unspoken.

'Yoo-hoo, folks! Lunch up!' Molly followed that with a coy question. 'Lucy, you're as red as half a dozen beetroots! Is that brother of mine misbehaving?'

'No,' I asserted, and then, since walls

or gardens here seemed to have ears anyway, I added, 'He was asking me to marry him over again.'

'Well! What a wonderful idea! It's the perfect answer to everything. Why didn't we think of it before? A nice little wedding, very quick and quiet. Matt will make the arrangements!'

I was being hustled and bustled. It was all happening much too fast. I tried to stop her, 'Please, just a moment. I haven't decided if I'll say yes.'

'But there's nothing to decide, is there? You're Mrs Devereux already! It's too late to start deciding yes or no, my love! Now as soon as Matt gets back I'll start him off on the arrangements. He fixed up your first wedding and he'll be delighted to do it again for you both.'

She stopped in full flow at the sound of a car pulling up at the house.

'Oh, good, that'll be Matt now!'

'No, it's not Matt,' Ralph said.

'It's not? Then who?'

I heard a car door shut, and footsteps. The unexpected caller said politely,

'As you're all in the garden I didn't go to the door, I hope you don't mind. Hello, again, Mr Devereux, you're certainly isolated out here — I took quite a while finding the house!'

Shaking like a leaf, too greatly shocked to speak, I was already out of my chair and stumbling along the rough path. As I pitched forward, two arms snatched me from falling. The voice that whispered, 'Take it easy!' was beyond mistaking.

For one moment Harvey held me, one moment of purest joy as I clung to him. A moment of wonder, perhaps not easy to explain to my husband and his family. But I relied on Harvey's ability to handle every situation, and I wasn't disappointed.

'It's nice to see Lucy looking well and getting more self-reliant. That's what I hoped to see,' he was saying to them. He added pleasantly, 'A pity all my patients haven't such a warm greeting for me!'

'Now I'm sure that's not the least bit

true, Doctor Sheridan!' Molly always overdid her welcomes. She went gushing on, 'So nice to meet you in person! And you'll stay for lunch with us? If only you'd let us know you were coming . . . '

His visit was a last-minute arrangement, Harvey explained, while back in my chair I listened and tried to believe this was real. He had taken a brief leave to come down to Cornwall, partly to see how I was progressing, partly to visit relatives who had just bought a cottage hereabouts. His aunt and uncle weren't expecting him either. With major renovations under way at their new home, they probably wouldn't even welcome him.

Molly could only repeat her lunch invitation, escorting him inside with fervent assurances about how pleased they were to have me here with them.

'I suppose,' Molly asked her guest brightly, 'you'll stay overnight with your relatives before you start back?'

'No, I daren't demand a bed while

they're in the throes of raging wood-worm. I'll find a hotel somewhere.'

I had hardly spoken so far, but now it was unthinkable to stay silent. I blurted out, 'Stay here! Please, stay here.'

'Oh, er, well.' Molly coughed dubiously. 'I don't quite know. It's sorting out the rooms, you see.'

'Molly, he can have my room! I'll share with Davina.'

It wasn't, of course, my house to be so free with, but I didn't care if my eagerness seemed odd. I wanted only to keep Harvey here as long as possible.

Molly coughed again, probably searching for some excuse.

'I really don't want to impose, Mrs Wilson,' Harvey murmured politely.

'Of course it's not imposing! If Lucy wants you to stay, of course you must stay,' she told him, not quite convincingly.

It was just settled when a car drew up, bringing Davina and her father to join us. Molly greeted him in some confusion. 'Thank goodness you're here, Matt, we've got company. Now can you guess who this is?'

He didn't guess, so introductions followed. He launched into a repeat of her protestations that it was so nice to meet someone who had helped me so much. He started on the catalogue of my progress.

'You certainly live in an interesting part of the country, Mr Wilson.' Harvey steered the conversation on to a different tack.

'If you fancy some exploring, there's a good walk to Mermaid Cove,' Matt was telling him. 'If you've finished lunch, I've a guide-book in the other room.'

I started to say I would like a walk, too, but Rita Greig intervened smartly.

'It's time for your afternoon rest, Mrs Devereux.'

'But I've rested all morning. I'm not a bit tired!'

'Don't forget you're only just on your feet after that bad chill.'

Upstairs, simmering with frustration,

I thought I heard Harvey setting out. In the quiet of my room, it seemed almost that this strange morning had been some sort of hallucination, all of it, from Ralph's second marriage suggestion to that wondrous moment when Harvey's voice brought my shadowed world to shining radiance.

'Lucy, dear? Are you asleep yet?' Molly was at the door, calling softly. 'Can we have a word before you settle down?'

I sighed in resignation as she plumped down on my bedside chair, a little breathless after climbing the stairs. If she wasn't overweight, she sounded it.

'Now first, promise not to take offence, only I've seen more of the world than you, and I'm almost old enough to be your mother.' It was an alarming preamble, but I didn't yet guess what was coming. 'Lucy, this Dr Sheridan of yours ... oh, a skilful doctor, I daresay, and he's helped you a lot, but also, he's a very attractive man.'

'Is he? I haven't ever seen him.'

'Oh, but you don't actually have to see him, it's his voice, his whole personality! And he knows how to make good use of it. Of course, I'd heard about it from my brother and Rita, but now I've met him myself. Lucy, remember when you first came to us, you were upset when we warned you about him?'

Indeed, I remembered. They had accused him of buttering up his wealthy patients for his own gain.

'If you're trying to say he . . . ' I choked on words I could scarcely speak.

'Please, let's keep calm,' she soothed. 'Believe me, Nurse Greig saw quite enough of that Hillside place to realise it specialises in lonely, ageing ladies whose health problems aren't so big as their bank balances. They're more than happy to have their poor foolish, old heads patted by our very dishy Dr Sheridan. You are heiress to quite a fortune, and — '

'That's enough! Don't say another

93

word!' I flared at her. 'Will you get out of my room, Mrs Wilson?'

'You're an heiress,' she went on firmly. 'You're an inexperienced young girl, and still a little sick and confused. Can't you understand, he won't let you slip through his fingers just because you're getting well? Answer me this, how many other ex-patients would he trail all this way to visit?'

'He has relatives near here, you heard him say so — '

'Oh, yes, the relatives. Whoever they are, doesn't he seem a lot more anxious to spend his time with you than with them?'

She patted my arm in reassurance as she stood up.

'When he leaves presently, just thank him for coming, but make it clear he needn't trouble himself again. All right, my love?'

★ ★ ★

Mermaid Cove, Harvey said later, was worth the long walk. Although you knew you were hearing just the tide trapped in the rocks, it would be easy to believe in the alluring voices of mermaids!

Everyone listened to him deferentially, whatever their private thoughts. Molly served up a fancy meal, Matt was a mine of information on local lore. I sat in a corner in silent frustration, because time was speeding past and there was no chance for us to be alone.

Of course, they discussed me, too. I was doing well in this short space of time, and it was even possible I might study music again. I had even made a small start already with Ralph's help.

'Go on, you two musicians,' Molly urged us. 'Let him hear your party-piece!'

Though I sensed Ralph was as reluctant as I was, we were dragooned to the piano.

What we produced encompassed some horrific errors, by no means all mine. Nevertheless, Harvey was full of praise.

'I wish I knew more about music. I've never had the time, unfortunately. But I believe Ralph is a real authority.'

'Oh, yes, before his hand was injured he won all sorts of prizes,' Molly enthused. 'He was going to study under Nicolai Someone in Paris. Weren't you, Ralphie?'

'Nicolas Belac,' Ralph supplied, 'years ago. It's not important now.'

'Are you sure about that? Give me that hand a moment.' Momentarily, authority was clear in Harvey's voice. 'Now grip mine. Hard. Harder!'

I heard from Ralph the involuntary gasp I had heard several times before.

'Bothers you quite a bit, does it?'

'Sometimes. It's not important.'

Harvey ended the examination with a tantalising, 'Uh-huh,' habitual to his kind. No-one mentioned the Anstey Vance Clinic. I needed to ask Harvey privately about that, just one of the many, many things I had to say to him.

And if he really wanted to, couldn't he have taken me aside from the listening ears? He made no attempt to do that. He asked me only impersonal questions, his manner friendly and kind but never more. It was just the same as when we spoke by telephone a few days ago, and disappointment stirred in me anew. Why had he bothered to come here at all, just to accept what the family wanted him to accept?

He sympathised with the adjustment problems of all of us, even taking their word that sometimes I made things worse by refusing their help. Not really my fault, they all agreed, just part of these hard days of rehabilitation after the terrible time the poor dear child had suffered.

Their poor dear child was already at a dangerous pitch of frustration when Rita ordered an early bedtime. It was the last straw.

I blazed at her, 'I'm not going to bed yet, and you can't make me!'

'Now don't let's have another scene, not in front of your visitor, dear.' It was a very patient and persuasive hand that took my arm. I didn't miss her meaningful *another*, implying all the trouble I frequently gave her.

'I'll go to bed when I'm good and ready!'

I heard a whisper from Ralph, 'Can't she stay longer if she wants?'

Miss Greig whispered back very audibly, 'Mr Devereux, you know it's not wise to give way to your wife.'

'That's right, early to bed and early to rise,' Molly said brightly. 'Say good-night, Lucy. Just go with Rita, my love, get a good night's sleep!'

'She's coming now, no problem,' Rita assured everyone as she finally hauled me to my feet.

I turned my face sharply away from Ralph's good-night kiss. Upstairs, finally left alone, I lay for a long time silently seething on my pillows, but really more unhappy than angry. Eventually, the sound of voices downstairs decided me. I groped for my dressing-gown.

I wouldn't be treated like a child! There was still time tonight for a heart-to-heart talk with Harvey. Once I was safely downstairs, they wouldn't shift me so easily a second time.

'Well, Mrs Devereux, and where do you think you're going?'

A voice from nowhere made me start violently. Had Rita Greig been sitting with her door open, ready to pounce? My nerves were set completely on edge by the thought that my every movement was being watched.

'You know you've a bell to ring if you need anything,' she said briskly. 'We don't want any accidents, so please don't wander about when you're half asleep.'

I was as awake as she was, but a retort died on my lips. What was the use? I let her steer me back to my bed.

It seemed more like a week than a night until dawn. Though I saw no morning light, I heard the chime of the clock downstairs, eventually the sound of Molly's slippers flip-flopping along the landing. Bubbling waterpipes, a distant radio, told me the house was awake. I knew quite clearly now what I would do.

'Well, you're an early bird!' Molly greeted me when I arrived below, decently dressed, I hoped.

There was an aroma of frying bacon and she was bustling busily about.

The next voice, over by the door, was unmistakable.

'Hello, Mrs Devereux. How are you this morning?'

I hoped and prayed no-one else was in earshot, but I had nothing to lose.

'I'm fine, thank you. But please, before you leave, I've got to talk to you alone! I can't stand much more — '

Harvey hushed me with a warning. 'Ssh! I know. Leave it to me.'

After that it was just a little easier to endure the ritual Sunday breakfast. That, too, seemed to last a week, with Matt talking on about the cricket results. Poor Davina, undoubtedly a clumsy child, overturned a milk-jug, and today was only mildly reproved by Molly.

'Never mind, darling, these things happen.'

When the chairs were pushed back and Molly began clattering plates, at long last my dwindling patience was rewarded.

Harvey announced that he had a minor problem with his car, and wanted to look at it before starting his journey.

'I'll come out to give you a hand in a moment,' Matt offered, but that indefinite moment would be enough.

I heard Harvey quietly instructing Davina, 'If you can bring Aunt Lucy outside, I've some presents hidden away in my car.'

'Presents? For me, too?'

'Especially for you!'

In hasty excitement, she hustled me out by the front door. It seemed that what he produced from the car was a set of books.

'On condition you read them all aloud to your Auntie. Will you do that for me?'

She agreed earnestly.

'Will you just wait here, Davina, and decide which she'd like best while Auntie and I go for a little stroll around?' Harvey said.

He took me out to the breezy cliff-top, the sun warm on my face, the familiar cries of the seabirds above, the tumble of water below.

I faltered, 'I've so much to tell you! I just haven't known what to do.'

'I know. That's why I fixed this weekend straight after your phone call.'

My story had to be told, and it began pouring out, much that I had told him already and now much more added. Though I struggled to be calm and coherent, my voice kept shaking. It shook most when I described Ralph's appeal to me yesterday in the garden.

'Another marriage ceremony, he said, because I still can't remember the first,' I wailed.

'You agreed with the plan?'

'I was going to, but then you arrived, and there wasn't a chance to settle anything. Oh, I know I'm being silly when we're married already.'

'But you'd rather decline. Have you considered another ceremony might help you regain your memory?'

'Yes! No! I don't know,' I mumbled.

Uncannily, he interpreted that confused answer.

'In your heart of hearts, you don't want to remember marrying Ralph. You were in love with him then, but you're not in love with him now, and you feel guilty about that. You'd rather it stayed forgotten. Am I right?'

I could have added more. I could have given him a very real and near reason why I couldn't fall in love with Ralph Devereux again.

I rushed on, bypassing the wedding plan.

'But can you wonder I don't want to be part of that family, if they're telling me lies and holding back my letters? Did Miss Aylmer write to me yet, do you know for sure?'

'I do know. She wrote several days

103

ago. I told her to say hello from me.'

'Then where did the letter go? Why haven't they told me? Oh, they keep me shut in this horrible house away from everyone, and I don't even know why they're doing it all!'

'You still don't know? You really don't?'

'I must be very stupid, but no, I don't!'

'Not stupid. Very honest, very trusting, very inexperienced about all the greed and envy in the world. You've never really been interested in your legacy, have you? You still feel everything belongs to your grandfather. But other people's minds don't usually work like that.'

We were sitting on scrubby grass, the blaze of sunshine tempered by the breeze off the sea. A bright and beautiful world was around me, all unseen.

I whispered, 'Please, just tell me straight out what you mean.'

'If I ask one question, perhaps you'll

understand. Has anyone ever made any sort of proposition about — well, how they can help you spend your money?'

His question did bring me new understanding. The Alvarez fortune, my legacy from the old man I had so quickly learned to love, certainly had brought me no happiness. It hadn't restored my precious sight, it had only deepened the darkness of my world if indeed everyone at The Cliff House aimed to wrest or persuade a large share of it from my hands.

And now, all at once, a horror came to me that so far was undreamed of. For was not Harvey voicing exactly the same accusations about the Wilsons as they had put forward against him? On both sides, there was not one atom of solid proof.

4

'I know this is very distressing for you, Lucy. I'm afraid I'm doing it badly.' Harvey's voice, low and warm, seemed full of concern. 'From all you've told me, and what I've seen since I arrived,' he was going on quietly, 'I can't dismiss everything as simply your imagination. Will you try to answer my question about the money? Will you think about it?'

'I'm sure no-one ever asked for a loan. I haven't even paid Matt and Molly for expenses, which would be only fair, but they wouldn't listen when I tried. Anyway,' I mused, 'they live here in this big house, and don't seem to have money troubles.'

'The house could be mortgaged up to its rafters. Or rented short term.'

'Oh, there is one thing,' I remembered suddenly. 'The Anstey Vance Clinic.'

'For Ralph? Whose bright idea was that?'

'Molly mentioned it, and Nurse Greig knew all about it. They said it was his last chance, only it would cost a lot, and it's best forgotten.'

Harvey gave a low sigh and went on, 'Yes, that sounds like an opening gambit. I think we can make a good guess at their plans. I'll try to explain, and you'll see it all adds up.'

As his voice went on, a muddled jigsaw began fitting neatly, ominously, into place. First, how the whole pattern of my life here, smothered with care and kindness yet constantly watched and disciplined, and especially denied all contact with the outside world, would soon make me utterly reliant on the family.

Secondly, a marriage ceremony would impress on me that Ralph was indeed my husband, and since I was sick and confused he should help me look after my fortune. No doubt he would take good care of his relatives who were stage-managing everything so efficiently.

107

'I suppose,' I faltered. 'Ralph married me for my money in the first place. He knew Grandfather was ill, and the car accident did most of the work for him straight off. Do you think Senor saw through him, and that's why he tried to stop the wedding?'

'It seems likely. I'm afraid I was never really sure of Ralph Devereux,' Harvey said soberly. 'He strikes me as a man with plenty to hide.'

But Ralph had been always kind, his voice and his touch so gentle, and he had loved and lost his world of music.

'However,' Harvey's voice cut through that stab of pain, 'we have to find some real proof first, before we can decide how to act.'

His use of the tiny word 'we' comforted me. I was no longer alone. And suddenly, without warning, tears came in an uncontrollable flood. They were racking, exhausting, and finally relieving.

Mutely I reached out outwards him, and my hand was gripped and held.

Then his arms were around me. His face was against mine, its touch a silent caress.

'I've missed you so much, you were so far away.' I heard my own voice struggling for words. 'Please, don't leave me alone here again. I can't stand any more. Take me with you when you go. I just want to be with you.'

'Don't rush things.' Harvey's quiet voice stilled me a little. 'You're lonely and frightened just now, but you need time to think . . . '

'Well, now, Doctor Sheridan.' I was shattered to hear another voice close by, an observer who had approached silently across the rough grass. 'That was interesting. Rather more interesting than ethical, wouldn't you say?'

Harvey had helped me to my feet, and I stood unsteadily, still clinging to him.

'Sorry to startle you.' Matt Wilson didn't sound at all sorry. 'But we were worried about Lucy. You forgot to tell us where you were taking her.'

'I told Davina we'd be back soon. I had something to discuss with Mrs Devereux.'

'I'm sure! I just heard, and saw, both of you discussing it.'

The accustomed quiet of Harvey's voice was taut now as I had never heard it before.

'I don't care for your tone, Mr Wilson. I'd advise you not to say any more!'

'You would? Well, that's too bad. There's a lot more it's my duty to say. I was prepared to give you the benefit of the doubt, but not any more. Lucy is part of my family, she's a sweet-natured, innocent girl and we're very fond of her. Heaven knows, she's had troubles enough without you bringing her a load more. So I intend to stop you, is that quite clear?'

'No, it's not!' Harvey's voice sharpened still more. 'Unless you have the brazen nerve to stand there and accuse me of . . .'

'Of what, Doctor?' Matt prompted.

'You're not usually lost for words. Is he, Ralph?'

I heard a mumble from Ralph. I hadn't known he was there with Matt. This was turning into a nightmare.

'Both Lucy's husband and I do have the brazen nerve, as you put it, to face the truth,' Matt was going on. 'We're quite ready to pass it on to the appropriate medical authorities. They'll want to hear about any members of your honoured profession dallying with wealthy married patients, I'm sure.'

I felt the hand holding mine grip hard.

'You have a mind like a sewer. Do you know that?' Harvey snapped.

'Not at all. I've just been doing my homework on you rather thoroughly. For instance, your reputation has a few cracks in it, eh? Wasn't there another time when your career nearly came unstuck? Wasn't there a young lady involved then as well? Do correct me if I'm wrong,' Matt invited silkily.

This time Harvey pulled his hand

free of mine. I groped for it in vain, and I realised he had started forward impulsively.

'The truth hurts, doesn't it?' Matt was saying. 'I believe you got away with your unprofessional conduct on that occasion. You were reprimanded, isn't that right? But I'm sure they won't be so lenient the second time around, Doctor Sheridan.'

I could hear my heart pounding. These dark insinuations were beyond all comprehending. I just cried out wildly, 'Ralph, stop them! Please, just stop them!'

It seemed he was already trying to do that. He appealed, low-voiced and desperately anxious, 'For God's sake, both of you! Remember, Lucy is here!'

'You'd better stand clear, Ralphie, before you get damaged,' his brother-in-law ordered him. 'If he wants to flatten me, let him do it!'

Never in my life had I felt so utterly helpless, unseeing, only hearing, and waiting in an agony of horror for the

112

sound of blows being struck. The fact that I heard none was due, it seemed, to Ralph's intervention. If indeed he was a weak and indecisive man, for once he acted with swiftness and strength, standing firm between the two adversaries until Harvey's first impulsive rage had cooled.

Then Ralph's hand took my arm, with equal firmness, to guide me back to the house. I believed he was genuinely appalled that such a scene had happened in my presence.

I went with him willingly, just thankful now to be looked after by anyone. Mostly there was heavy silence between us, until I had to ask him, 'Are they coming? What are they doing?'

He told me Matt was hurrying on ahead, Harvey following us at a distance. I kept expecting Ralph to say something about finding me, his wife, in the arms of another man; for surely this was his ideal chance to play the heartbroken but forgiving martyr, so making me deeply remorseful, and maybe more generous with the benefits I could bring to him and his conniving family?

But perhaps he just felt it safer to wait till Harvey was gone. They intended my parting with Harvey to be a final one, by whatever means. I was still numb with the horror of Matt's insinuations, that something had happened in Harvey's past, there was some ugly flaw in the reputation of the man who commanded respect in all who knew him — and in me an emotion far deeper than that.

'Ralph!' I forced myself at last to speak. 'I must know the truth, about those horrible lies Matt was telling just now!'

'Not lies, I'm afraid.'

'Then tell me! I have to know!'

'The man isn't all he seems, I'm afraid.'

'Then he's certainly not the only one around here!' I said bitterly.

His hold on me loosened. We were safely on the driveway now, and I pulled myself free.

'I can find my own way! I'm getting more independent every day, haven't you all told Harvey that fifty times over?'

It was sheer luck that I blundered into Harvey's car, where earlier he had given Davina her present. I grabbed hold of the door, determined to stay put until I could speak to him again. Vaguely I was aware of movements and voices, even more of the tensely-charged atmosphere.

'Lucy, what are you doing still out here?' That was Harvey's voice right beside me, and he was throwing his things into the back of the car, obviously still seething with anger.

'I'm waiting for you,' I said simply, and then rushed on. 'Listen, I've changed my mind about going back with you to Hillside! And please, you mustn't come here again! Promise me you won't.'

'I expected you'd say that,' he said abruptly. He knew me so well. 'You really think I care what a few

115

unpleasant-minded people believe?'

'You know it's more than that. They could harm you if we give them a chance, and harm your work, and that's so important. Please promise me, Doctor Sheridan!'

He corrected me, even more abruptly, 'Harvey!'

'Harvey,' I whispered. 'You've helped me so much already. I do understand now what's going on here, and I'll find some real proof, and then I'll face them with it.'

'You have a lot of courage, do you know that?' The tremble in his voice almost defeated all my struggles for composure.

'Not really. I just can't bear to make trouble for you.'

'Lucy, it's nice that you trust me so much.' His voice was steady again, but very low. 'It's nice, it's very flattering. But . . .'

There was no chance to complete that sentence. We were no longer alone. Matt was saying in his usual level tones,

'Isn't it about time you left, Doctor?'

Neither of us answered him. Harvey asked me just one more question.

'You're quite sure you know what you're doing?'

'I'm sure! Just go,' I begged, 'before things get any worse.'

They were the last words. The car door shut. I stood bereft and alone, listening to the tyres move on the gravel.

'You'd better come inside, Mrs Devereux.' A sickly aroma of spearmint announced Nurse Greig, and she took my arm firmly.

* * *

'Are you awake?' an anxious voice asked.

After everything, I wasn't back in the house. I had managed to compromise with a sheltered part of the garden, a bench in the shade.

'Auntie, are you awake? Quick, while no-one's about!'

Davina landed herself beside me, and I felt something being thrust into my hand.

'Take it! He left it for you, that nice doctor left it. It's an envelope addressed to him with a stamp on it, and if you want to go back to the nursing home, I've got to post it and he'll fetch you, see? It's our secret, he said. I swore I wouldn't tell, even if they torture me with red-hot knives!'

I was speechless, drowned in a huge tide of relief. How could I ever have doubted Harvey's caring even for one instant?

'You've got to hide it. Sleep with it under your pillow, that's what I do with things!' Davina's excited voice was suddenly wistful. 'If you do go there, can I go with you?'

'Davina, darling,' I whispered, and then again my voice failed.

I put my hands over my face to hide welling tears.

She wriggled beside me.

'If you don't want me to come, it doesn't matter.'

'Of course I want you! Of course I do.'

I lifted my head, anxious to comfort her, my eyes wide open.

It was a vivid, brilliant flash of light that made me flinch back as though I had been struck. And then I was looking into a child's small, pale, woebegone face. Merciful heaven, truly a human face, dappled by shaded sunlight, the most beautiful face in all the world! Was it a dream, a mirage, or was I going out of my mind? So clear, this sad, little face, and around it a whole glory of daylight, a glowing world of shapes and colours!

Davina's scared blue eyes stared back into mine, pretty blue eyes behind dark-rimmed glasses. I wanted to cry aloud, *Don't be afraid, I can see you!* It was some strange instinct that held me silent.

'Auntie?' Her voice reached me again across the delirium of light. 'What is it? What's wrong with you?'

Every pulse in my body was racing in

a wild exultation. For her sake more than mine, I struggled to be calm. There was no chance to answer her. Someone else had approached across the grass from the house behind us.

'Run away and play, Davina,' Molly ordered her impatiently. 'Haven't I told you over and over not to pester Auntie when she's resting? Lucy, I've just made some coffee. Will you come in with me?'

It was again pure instinct that guided me. I resisted the almost overwhelming urge to look for the first time at my sister-in-law, and just stared ahead at a blur of leaves and grass. If I could feign continued blindness, it was a heaven-sent chance to outwit these people, to discover the truth! Had I the strength to conceal and use this miracle that had been granted me?

While Molly escorted me to the house, with more of those effusive assurances, I managed stolen glimpses of a large, badly-kept but still pleasant garden, and then there loomed a spreading bulk of grey stone, mellowed by many years of sea winds.

It was so very strange that the house I had thought a forbidding prison should lie here basking peacefully in the sunshine. Tubs of flowers stood around the door, more blooms were massed in green window-boxes.

The armchair was covered in faded chintz, among others grouped round a stone fireplace. I saw leaf-green patterned carpets, curtains stirring at an open window. A tray of cups waited on a polished wood table, beside a bowl of bright yellow roses. After the garden it was very cool, very dim.

I let Molly's voice flow over me while she poured the fragrant coffee. I had been a little wrong about Mrs Wilson. She was much younger than I had thought, with thick, wavy dark hair pulled back in a loose knot.

'Here, Nurse, would you give Lucy hers, dear?' she requested.

I was not wrong about Nurse Greig. Beanpole slim in black trousers and a blue uniform-tunic, her dark hair was severely cropped, her face was sharp in contour, with the mouth lacking warmth or humour. Yes, I had known she looked like this. And deep in my mind, an amazing spark of memory flickered to life. Of course I had known, because I had seen her face before — on the day I was almost run over in the village, the day I dreamed Rita Greig and Ralph were talking beside my bed! It had been no dream, but the first brief glimmer of returning sight.

But on that day, the light had soon faded again. And so my mind raced desperately on, maybe, even now, were the shadows gathering ready to close in once more?

I must not waste one precious second of vision.

I said shakily, 'I can't drink this, I don't feel well.' It was a very simple way of testing whether these pleasant surroundings were still a cage.

I said again, quite truthfully, 'My head is spinning. I want to go to a doctor. There must be one in St Dawes. Please take me in the car.'

'Dear, dear. Well . . . ' Molly uttered uncertainly.

'Please take me, or ask Matt to take me. Please.'

Molly coughed, and I saw her look across at Rita as she tried to soothe me. 'You're just upset, that's all. Just have a nice lie-down.'

'I don't want to lie down!' I insisted quite aggressively. 'Haven't I a right to see a doctor if I want?'

Again Molly's questioning dark eyes turned towards Rita, and this time I saw Rita shake her head. A whole language of looks and signals had been going on around me all this while!

Through the window, with its billow of curtains, was a blur of green that was the garden, and I could make out two figures walking down a path in deep discussion. The faces weren't clear, but Ralph must be one of them, and the taller man, thickset and balding, with a glimmer of spectacles, could only be

Matt. There came to me the shattering thought that if this blessed vision had dawned an hour sooner, I would have seen Harvey . . .

'Molly!' I hailed her again, rather desperately now. 'I want to know exactly what your husband found out about Harvey.'

'She was some sort of showgirl he was involved with, a dancer. French, Gabrielle someone. Matt has some news cuttings. The girl had a sick husband who was quite wealthy. Oh, it's not a pretty story, trying to muscle in on a dying man's wife and his money. But Dr Sheridan didn't succeed, and he got back from Paris to face those medical disciplinary people. There were other things, too.'

'Gross negligence to his patients, for a start,' Rita put in.

Molly hushed her hastily saying, 'Lucy, dear, we weren't going to worry you with any of it, but perhaps really it's best out in the open.'

Still I was silent, her voice coming

across a great space. The dim room was becoming dimmer, the green curtains and yellow roses fading. For me, night came at noon.

My bedroom door opened, quite late in the evening. 'Aunt Lucy, can you wake up a minute?' Davina whispered.

She was sniffing even more than usual. She had been crying recently.

'I'm awake! What's wrong?'

'I hate them! All of them! They found the books he gave us and they said we can't keep them. I shouldn't take presents from people I don't know.'

'Ssh! We'll keep them. I'll make sure it's all right,' I promised.

'Will you really?' The bed bounced as she planted herself on the edge. 'They sent me to bed without supper!'

'Don't worry, we'll fix it tomorrow.'

She seemed to accept that. Still sniffling, she mumbled, 'You're always nice to me, and no-one else is, not ever! And I've been so worried about you all day. Ever since this morning in the garden, you looked sort of strange!'

'Did I look strange?'

'You looked as if you could see me.'

For a moment I was quiet. I wanted desperately to confide in her, because she was my sole ally here. But how could I burden the child with such a secret, and expect her to aid and abet me?

'I can't see you, Davina,' I said. 'Darling, I only wish I could.'

I didn't feel better the next day, nor the tomorrows that followed; a heaviness of depression weighed me down, and there was no-one to share its burden. Every day, every hour, my thoughts drifted across the miles to Harvey. I longed to hear his voice, to hear him explain that those unpleasant stories about him were a distinctive distortion of the truth.

I asked if I could send a letter to old Miss Aylmer at Hillside, and by an astonishing coincidence, after Molly had vaguely agreed to that, the next day she presented me with an envelope.

'For you, my love! It's handwritten. I

wonder if it's from your friend,' she gushed helpfully. 'Shall I read it? Oh, such a pretty card she's sent! . . . '

'Hello, Lucia', she read out, '*I do hope you are well. I'm much better and going for a holiday with my nephew in his caravan. Sorry I can't give you an address but I'll write again some time. Love from your friend, Miss Aylmer.*'

I thanked Molly and took the card upstairs, to ask Davina to read it over again.

'Hello, Lucia, *I do hope you are well* . . . ' she started off, just the same words, just the same. But Miss Aylmer never, never had called me Lucia. Wasn't it always 'Lucy dear?'

Davina giggled when I held the card close to my face, and said I was sniffing it like a rabbit. I could detect not the faintest hint of the lavender water that Miss Aylmer lived and breathed.

Sometime later, somehow, the card went missing from my room.

That episode was just one thing. I

also kept asking if I could visit my grandfather's London solicitor, Mr Gudge, as there were things I needed to clear up, and I could go by train if Nurse Greig came with me. There was always a good excuse for not going anywhere at present.

I thought with bitterness, if I proposed a trip to arrange access for them to my bank account, the routine response, 'In a while when you're stronger,' would change quite suddenly to an urgent, 'Right, let's go!'

All this while there was repeated pressure about the second marriage. Molly tried to tempt me by describing a honeymoon in a tropical paradise, which doubtless I would be expected to pay for. I did notice that Ralph left all the persuading to her. He seemed to be avoiding me, spending his time roving the surrounding countryside, or shut in his room playing piano recordings. As Harvey once said, he seemed an unhappy, haunted man.

On the Friday of that miserable

week, I lacked even Davina's company, for Molly and Rita went off in Rita's car to the nearest town, taking a sulky, protesting Davina with them. I was left in the sole charge of Ralph.

I lay listlessly on my bed, remembering for the thousandth time a stolen glimpse of overgrown flower-borders and a grey stone house; and as well, another magical instant of sight, that had seemed just a dream at the time but now I knew better.

It had been this same room, Nurse Greig straightening my bed and hissing across the room to the shadowy presence of my anxious husband, 'For goodness' sake, Ralphie! Are you the qualified nurse, or am I? . . . '

I sat up suddenly, shaking as though an ice-cold torrent had enveloped me. 'Ralphie', she called him! Ralphie.

Not the formal Mr Devereux she used in my presence! Not even a more friendly Ralph while I was safely asleep. No, this was the pet name only his family used. Surely a strange form of address from employee to employer, especially from a semi-stranger newly resident under his roof?

At long last, was this really the first concrete foundation of the proof I sought? Was Rita Greig on far closer terms with all of them than anyone wanted me to know?

When the first shock of discovery abated just a little, I knew quite clearly what I must do. Under the lining-paper of a drawer was a certain stamped envelope. I could feel the edges of the stamp, and though I couldn't feel the address below, I knew it was there — Harvey's address.

I had to tell him this. I would cause him no trouble, ask no active help. One innocent little note surely could bring no difficult consequences? Among some of Davina's things left in my room were pencils and paper, and I sat down to force my thoughts to clarity and my fingers to work. Even though the scribbled lines jumbled together, there must be something legible.

The pencil raced, the words flowed, and I sealed the envelope. While only Ralph was here, I could slip out of the house. At this moment I had no thought for anything but getting to the village, somehow following the lane to the bus route, hitch-hiking, simply walking, so I could drop my precious letter in a post-box.

I went downstairs, a now well-practised hand holding my white cane. Halfway down I heard a car pull up, the door bang. If Rita and Molly had returned, my chance was gone. Yet it didn't sound like Rita's car.

The front door stood open, letting in a strong breeze, and Ralph was talking to someone just outside. I tapped my way out of the house.

'Lucy, it's all right.' He was quickly beside me, his hand taking mine. 'These people took a wrong turning. They're looking for Mermaid Cove. Oh, this is my wife,' his soft voice introduced me.

A woman's voice, a staid, severe,

elderly-sounding voice, acknowledged politely, 'How do you do? Sorry to be a nuisance. My husband didn't bring the map, did you, Brad?'

Just an ordinary, everyday pair of tourists. For me their intrusion was heaven sent.

'Ralph, isn't there that guide book of Matt's?' I struggled to steady my voice. 'Couldn't you fetch that?'

He hesitated, as always. It wasn't till Brad prompted, 'That would be a help,' that he withdrew.

Even then he warned me first, 'Stay still, because the hose is loose all over the path. Do be careful, Lucy.'

I did stay still and silent, till I heard a sound at the front door that meant he had gone in. Then I tugged the letter from my pocket and thrust it towards the unseen strangers.

'Please, would you do something for me? You are still there?'

'We're both here,' the severe-voiced lady confirmed.

'You'll have realised I can't see you.

This is an extremely important letter I want posted, and I'd be so grateful if — '

I needed to go no further. A hand brushed mine and took the envelope. But before I could speak my thanks, the woman said, 'There's no address on this. It's blank.'

'No address? There is! He wrote it for me himself.'

'You're mistaken. The envelope is blank.'

Disbelief changed to surging anger. Someone had searched my room after Harvey's visit. Someone had sifted through my belongings and substituted a plain envelope for the addressed one. Helpless innocent that I was, I would have sent it on its way in blissful ignorance, never knowing that he failed to receive it.

'Then will you fill in the address for me? It's to Dr H. Sheridan at Hillside View Nursing Home . . . '

Again, I got no further. Again, the stranger halted my words.

'We know the rest, thank you. And we know Harvey can do without your letters, young lady!'

A supporting hand held my arm. With the world spinning round, I must have looked about to collapse on the gravel path. But after a moment I shook myself free. The woman was asking, 'Are you all right, Mrs Devereux? I'm sorry, there's no easy way to do this.'

'Who are you?' I whispered. 'Tell me who you are!'

It was her husband who answered.

'Our name is Stanford. We're Harvey's aunt and uncle. We recently moved to a place a few miles from here.'

A morsel of sane thought returned to me.

'I know, you're the relatives with woodworm!'

Mrs Stanford coughed. 'You've evidently heard of us. Did Harvey also tell you why he's more of a son to us than a nephew?'

'No.' I shook my head blankly. 'He didn't say.'

'Harvey was orphaned when he was a very small child, just a baby. We took him in. We weren't able to have children of our own, so we brought him up as our son. Do you understand?'

This much I did understand, that Harvey had been sadly bereaved in childhood just as I was, a bond between us I had never known. Only, in my case there had been my Grandfather Alvarez, a far-off figure footing the bills for my care and education, whereas Harvey must have known all the love the Stanfords could give him.

But there was little kindness now in Mr Stanford's slow, heavy voice.

'You realise now this wasn't just a chance call. We came here for a purpose.' He cleared his throat harshly. 'We have something to say to you. We're sorry about your sad affliction — '

'But that hardly enters into it.' His wife took up the story in her staccato bursts. 'You have a beautiful home.

135

You're a very wealthy girl. You're the wife of a highly presentable young man, and we've just seen how he's devoted to you. So for pity's sake, leave Harvey alone. The last thing in the world he wants is an entanglement with the likes of you.'

I tried to speak, but no words would come.

She swept on, 'And it looks as though we're just in time to nip things in the bud. This letter of yours, we definitely won't be sending it.'

It was then that sudden horror seized me. I put out my hand to regain the envelope. I groped in space for it, and my hand remained empty.

'No, I'm not giving it back to you,' the stern voice said. 'I shall pass it over to your husband, Mrs Devereux!'

5

Ralph said quietly, 'Yes, I see.' Quiet as he always was quiet, though at this moment you might expect fires of anger or depths of hurt.

Chiefly Mrs Stanford, with a few grunts of agreement from her husband, had just dutifully informed him that they had confiscated my secret letter, meant to be despatched in cloak-and-dagger fashion to their nephew; a liaison not just showing gross disloyalty on my part, but conceivably ruinous for Harvey Sheridan.

Horrified and humiliated, I stood hanging on to the front door, trying to recall exactly what I had written to Harvey. I knew only that those few scribbled lines had been intended for no other eyes than his.

'Well,' Mrs Stanford prompted Ralph impatiently, 'you'll read it, of course?'

The next sound that came to me was a sharp ripping of paper, and a startled, 'Bless my soul!' from Harvey's uncle.

'Well, that was silly!' Mrs Stanford left no-one in doubt of her feelings. 'We didn't give you that letter to tear up without even looking at it. How shall we know now if they're arranging to meet somewhere?'

'We won't know,' Ralph answered her. 'I'm sorry, but this is Lucy's private correspondence. I've no right to read her letters.'

'You're her husband, aren't you?'

'Anything Lucy wants to do, she can do.' Still so quietly, Ralph answered that outraged demand.

For once, Mrs Stanford seemed lost for words as Ralph added, 'I'm sure you meant well, but this is my business and Lucy's, not yours.'

It was amazing to hear Ralph, of all people, telling someone to mind their own business. I could hardly believe it.

'Come on, Daphne, we've heard enough,' Mr Stanford urged his wife gruffly. 'It's obvious our help and advice aren't welcome here.'

Car doors shut rather forcibly. The engine started. Tyres moved on the gravel. I stood still, trembling with shock, and with relief that these people had gone. But that relief was short-lived. Ralph was saying, 'I think it's time we had a serious talk. Let's go inside.'

I sat in the same armchair where, a few days ago, I looked around in wonder at chintzy chair-covers and a stone fireplace. Today, all of it was a void. A clock somewhere ticked heavily. I felt Ralph's unseen eyes watching me.

It might have been easier if he stormed and raged at what would seem to be my blatant infidelity. But he sounded every bit as nervous as I was.

'Are you in love with him? Are you, Lucy?'

It was something I had never dared ask myself. I had been scared even to start thinking it through.

I stammered, 'I don't know.'

'I think you do know. Please, just tell me the truth.'

'Well,' I floundered, and then all at once the words came. 'I know this much. Sometimes, after the accident, I didn't want to wake up another morning, to go on living at all, but Harvey showed me how to find the world again. And I'll remember him as long as I live, every word he's ever said to me, and how he said it. So if that's loving, yes, I do love him. Is that what you want me to say?'

The impassioned words trailed off there. I heard Ralph sigh, but then the silence lasted so long that I burst out, 'All right, I've told you, so what will you do about it? I love him, and I'm married to you. But you don't even seem angry!'

'I could never be angry with you. Don't you know that?'

The words quietened me. He went on softly, not very steadily, 'And I'd like to tell you, if you want to go back to the nursing home, or anywhere else to be near him, you're free to go. I want you to be happy, that's all I want. Can you understand what I'm saying?'

I understood the words, indeed. But the motive behind them was as veiled as his still unknown face. He was part of the conspiracy going on around me, and I could never trust him, not his gentle touch nor his appealing voice. It seemed, at this moment, that he was the greatest hypocrite of them all.

'Do you understand?' he repeated. 'You're free, if you want to be free. I won't stand in your way. Only for your own sake, please do make quite sure first that this man is really worth so much of your devotion.'

He got no further than that. The Alvarez temper reared its fiery head, and I exploded at him.

'Don't tell me what he is or isn't worth, you of all people! Not when he's achieved more already than you ever will in your whole lifetime! Oh, maybe he's had troubles, and he even did something he's ashamed of. But whatever it was, whatever it cost him, he'll still go on working himself into the ground for people who need his help, while you wallow in your self-pity and hang on the coat-tails of your horrible family, and let them use you however they want!'

'That's not fair!'

The words were a cry of pain, but I was beyond being moved by them.

'All right, you lost your dream and that was tragic, but if you were half the man Harvey is, you'd have made a new start. You could have taught music, helped people who'd be thrilled to have your help. But no, you just gave up. So I despise you, I wish I'd never married you! And it's not just because I know you're all itching to get hold of poor Senor's legacy, it's because of what you're doing to Harvey, to get him safely out of the way while you all grab all you can get from me!'

I didn't wait for him to answer. I

made a dive for where the door should be.

My dramatic words, my sweeping exit, were rather spoiled as I tripped on something and lurched forward completely off-balance. I would have fallen if Ralph hadn't caught and held me. For a moment I was glad of the timely rescuing arms. But as my fright faded, I realised the close embrace wasn't fading along with it.

Vainly I tried to struggle free, and then he kissed me, his lips full on mine. I twisted my head away, wrenching my mouth from his. Still his searching lips sought my eyes, my forehead, my hair.

There was just one thing I could do. I hit out quite wildly. My hand struck him in the face with stinging force.

'Sorry,' I mumbled, 'but don't do that! Don't ever do that!'

He was silent, no longer holding me. I stumbled away from him, and upstairs to my room.

★　★　★

Rather earlier than usual, Matt arrived home that Friday evening. Several hours had dragged by in the sanctuary of my room.

I told Rita and Molly when they came in that I had a headache, a lame enough excuse but it sufficed. Downstairs, I well knew, Ralph would be describing the visit from Harvey's relatives. They would be discussing how to deal with any more interference.

Very cautiously I inched my door open. The floorboards creaked, my legs were like rubber, but I kept on going. Clinging to the rail, scarcely breathing, I glided from stair to unseen stair. Below, noisy music wafted across the hall, but there were voices as well, not pausing at my approach.

'Here you are, more from the credit card people, overdue bills, and, yes, another letter from that bank.' That was Molly, sharp and complaining, quite devoid of her usual effusive sweetness.

Was that questioning letter from the bank actually addressed to Mrs Lucia

Devereux, wondering at my silence? If I knew that for sure, I would need no more proof. I heard Matt seeming to muse over it.

'Hmm . . . yes . . . well, I'll keep stalling him. Don't worry about it.'

'I do worry!' Molly still fretted. 'We've had more trouble here today, haven't we, Rita? I don't know how much more I can take. Running around after that kid, and she has the foulest temper when she gets going.'

I didn't delude myself. 'That kid,' of course, was me.

'Matt,' she was insisting, 'how much longer must we put up with this?'

'Not much longer,' his smooth voice reassured her. 'We're nearly there.'

'Well, I hope you're right. I never expected it would take as long as this — '

There he stopped her short, his warning cough probably accompanying urgent hand signals. I heard my name.

'Here's Lucy, creeping about like a little ghost. How are you feeling, my dear? I was so sorry to hear you weren't too well today.'

Such cordial welcomes Matt always gave me. Or they were at face value.

Molly, no longer sharp and aggrieved but again exuding sweetness, ushered me in to supper. I had to sit where she put me, even though it was on the sofa beside Ralph. Briefly I was reassured by Davina perching near me, but she was soon banished to her bed.

I wished now I had stayed in my room. Today had stretched my endurance near to breaking point.

'I'm glad you're better,' Matt was saying to me, 'because I've some good news for you and Ralphie!'

He was sitting at the table for his meal, and the smell of the hot food sickened me. The house seemed charged with the airless foreboding of thunder that had threatened all day. I had always hated storms.

'Yes, you'll like a trip in the car, Lucy. I've made an appointment for tomorrow with Mr Pengowan. That's

Reverend Edward Pengowan. His church is just outside St Dawes. He was most helpful when I explained the position.'

'Tomorrow?' I said dully.

'Dearie me, you're still half asleep!' Molly chided. 'It's your wedding Matt is talking about. Of course, Mr Pengowan wants to see you both first, then the date can be fixed. As soon as possible, Matt?'

'Yes, indeed. The sooner the better. Mr Pengowan hopes like we all do that the ceremony itself will restore Lucy's memory. But even if it doesn't, she'll be rid of this half-life of hers. She'll really feel one of the family.'

I could hear now an ominous roll of thunder. The blank darkness of the room that concealed watching eyes, scheming and mocking eyes, was closing in on me. I forced my dry lips to speak.

'But, I don't want . . . '

'What don't you want?' Matt asked with kindly patience. 'Don't worry, just leave it all to us. All you need do is be a pretty bride for a second time.'

It was then that something seemed to snap in my head. I cried out quite wildly, 'I don't want to feel one of your family! I don't want to be a bride again, I wish I'd never married Ralph the first time. He knows that, I've told him. And you're all just as bad as each other, all plotting behind my back, pretending to be kind when it's only to get at my grandfather's money! That's why I'm really here, isn't it? Isn't it?'

I had said far too much. So what could it matter if the rest poured out?

'Well, you're not fooling me so easily. You won't get one penny from me. Not Ralph, not any of you! Not unless,' I finished in breathless, bitter passion, 'not unless it's over my dead body!'

For a moment the silence in the room was as heavily oppressive as the rising storm outside. Molly said at last, rather shakily, 'She doesn't know what she's saying, poor love. She's hysterical.'

'Hardly surprising, with this building

up in her mind all this time.' Matt's voice was sterner than usual. 'And I can guess how it all started.'

I heard him leave his seat at the table. His two hands caught mine and held them captive, despite all my struggles. I couldn't shut out his persuasive words.

'Lucy, listen to me. No, just stay still, try to be calm. Listen to me.'

There was something hypnotic in those soothing repetitions. Still resisting weakly, I had to listen.

'That's better,' he approved. 'Now let's discuss this quietly. We're not angry, my dear. We know it's not your fault. Wasn't it Dr Sheridan who put all these ideas in your head?'

'No!' I still defied him. 'I knew something was going on here. He just explained it all to me, that's all!'

'I'm sure he did. Lucy, it's been proved publicly before that the man is a fortune-hunter. Isn't it obvious to you that he's trying to turn you against us for his own ends?'

'Of course he is,' Molly put in

149

earnestly. 'Once he gets you distrusting your own family and relying on him, he's well on his way to making himself a rich man. Didn't I warn you before, if anyone's angling for your poor grandad's money it's that two-faced Don Juan of a doctor? Matt, how can we make her believe us? She'll make herself ill like this!'

'She's already ill, I'm afraid,' Matt said quietly. 'That's the whole basis of his campaign. Those critical head injuries she suffered in the accident — correct me if I'm wrong, Nurse?'

Rita spoke up quickly. 'You're absolutely right, Mr Wilson. In her confused mental state, and obviously a doctor would understand that more than anyone, it would be quite easy to induce a persecution complex, make her think everyone is her enemy. Everyone except himself, of course!'

I tore my hands free at last. Furiously I protested.

'I lost my temper just now, but

there's nothing at all wrong with my mental state.'

'No?' Matt said gently. 'When you can't remember marrying your husband?'

I had no answer. I couldn't stop the world disintegrating around me, fantasy and reality becoming one.

'The envelope Harvey gave me, someone changed it,' I accused. 'You can't deny that!'

'I did it,' Molly admitted with shattering candour. 'When I was putting away your laundry I found it. I couldn't upset you by just destroying it, making you search and search, so I put another one there. I hoped and prayed you'd never try to send it. I had to do it, Lucy, for your own good.'

'All right, tell me something else. Nurse Greig called Ralph 'Ralphie' when they thought I couldn't hear.'

It was Matt who answered this time.

'It's a wonder that hasn't happened more often. The answer is very simple. When Ralph had some treatment for

151

his hand at St Paul's Hospital, Rita was training there and they got to know each other. That's why we were delighted when Rita, of all people, answered our advert for a nurse. Only we felt it best to keep things very formal. It wouldn't have helped you to find your husband had an old flame on the premises, a girl he knew before he met you.'

'That's right,' Molly chimed in again. 'If only you'd talked to us before, my love, we could have set your poor mind at rest.'

Words, words, words. I was adrift among them, they ebbed and flowed and swirled, engulfing me in their whirlpools of fear and doubt. And before I could surface, there came a still greater terror. A huge crash of sound seemed to tear the whole world apart, making me scream aloud again and again in nameless dread.

Immediately there were arms around me, the warmth of a face was against mine, the same face I had struck a while ago in anger and contempt. Now, I needed help even from him.

He was whispering that it was just a thunderstorm, but I couldn't make sense of the words. There were other voices and movements as well, a cup was being held to my lips.

In my clumsiness I spilled more than I drank. Cloying drowsiness brought me a blessed calm.

'Go to sleep,' the voices said. 'You're sick, Lucy, but we'll help you. Just trust us, just go to sleep.'

★   ★   ★

After the storm, the morning air was pure and fresh. My window was open to the breeze. I raised myself on my pillow, my throat parched, but my thoughts clear as the sweet, cleansed air.

It was fortunate they were, for around my bed was not the familiar pall of blankness, but neither, alas, the radiance of daylight. This was something I hadn't known before, a phantom world of blurred shapes, an eerie twilight of shadows.

I could make out the bulk of surrounding furniture, even my dressing-gown draped over a chair. A shimmer of extra brightness must be the window. They had drugged me. Of course, that was the answer. With my wild questions and wilder accusations, my hysteria born of long overstrain and a violent clap of thunder, I had been such a nuisance that they gave me some sort of sedative, and very nearly had me convinced that everything was a delusion of my own wandering mind.

It wasn't wandering now. With complete clarity I recalled a moment preceding all that frenzy, when I eavesdropped on an opened letter being passed from hand to hand. It came from the bank manager that Matt had promised to keep on stalling.

I remembered just as clearly Molly's shrill complaints.

'I don't know how much more I can take! Matt, how much longer?'

I could still hear her husband's ever-smooth answer, 'Not much longer, we're nearly there.'

Not much longer! Did he mean, not much longer to stall bank officials or legal men anxious to arrange my business affairs? Did he mean, not much longer to suffer my presence in their home?

Last night they gave me only a harmless sedative to make me sleep, but it need not have been harmless.

It was so very obvious now. All this while I must have been doubly blind not to perceive the appalling truth. For why would these people prolong their tedium of caring for a tiresome invalid, why plot and plan to extract the Alvarez fortune from me in dribs and drabs, when one small accident would deliver it into the inheriting hands of my husband? . . .

Through the nightmare that had seized me, I heard footsteps along to my door. I saw the door opening.

'You're awake!' Molly's bright voice,

Molly's plump form a blur of pale blue. 'Feeling better after that nice long sleep? It was the storm upset you. I hate them, too. Here you are, I knew you'd like your breakfast.'

I couldn't speak to her, but she seemed not to mind, nor even notice. Fussing with the tray, she chattered all the time.

'Eat it up, we've got to build up your strength. It's a beautiful day. Matt's just getting the car ready. You'll enjoy a little drive, won't you? But finish every bit of that breakfast first.'

I shrank from the touch of her hands, the jarring of her voice. Still and silent I waited until the door shut behind her.

The tray she had left, the tempting aroma of coffee, seemed so very innocent yet could be so lethal.

I could eat nothing, drink nothing, ever again, in this house. I had to get away from here, away from these people. I had to get away!

Soon I was dressed and ready. Half feeling, half seeing, listening for every smallest sound, I started downstairs.

It was only a few steps down, amid tiers of banister and a sea of dark carpet, that I suddenly stopped. At the bend of the stairs a mirror was mounted on the wall, and a face gazed back at me from the glass, an oval-shaped, small-featured face with huge, luminously jet-black eyes against its unnaturally pale skin. A vision of myself which held me in shocked fascination, until I remembered there might be someone watching from below.

A moment after, I paused again, this time because Molly's vacuum cleaner had been left sprawled across a stair. I saw it, so I didn't fall headlong to the bottom of the flight. If I had fallen, it would surely be passed off as a momentary lapse by an overstressed housekeeper.

'Be careful!' Matt warned me of the obstacle I was already past. 'Good gracious, Molly should know better. I'll have a little word with her. Let me help you, Lucy.'

His hand on mine made me shudder. But for once it wasn't a hand in the darkness. My shadowy sight revealed his face, quite near to my own, and it was no stranger's face. I had seen it before, somewhere, sometime.

I dared not look at him more closely. And it wouldn't have helped much, because already the shadows were deepening again.

Downstairs there was a dim room peopled by elusive, moving silhouettes. I was given a chair, and told we would leave soon for our important date with Reverend Pengowan. I sat quite still. No-one must guess I fully understood now the dangers all around me.

Only Harvey Sheridan could confirm my story. Only Harvey could convince everyone of the truth. Never had I needed him so much.

'Lucy?' Ralph's soft voice was saying beside me. 'You look so pale, are you sure you're well enough to go out? Shall we go another day?'

You're in this, too, Ralph, I answered

silently, fiercely, in my mind. You didn't rescue me from that scene last night. You held me while I drank whatever I drank.

'Oh, she's just in a dream this morning,' Molly was asserting brightly. 'Lucy, Matt brought in some chocolates last night, especially for you, the kind you like. Go on, try one now.'

I stood up.

'No, not just now. Is Davina in the garden? I think I'll go and find her.'

'Yes, do that,' Molly agreed. 'Mind how you go.'

I had no coat, and no time to fetch one. I had the clothes I wore, and my white cane, and my handbag, if they had left any money in it. There was no time to find that out either. I found the front door ajar, and the brightness of sun on rain-washed grass dazzled me. Was the door standing open because they had booby-trapped the path?

'Auntie!' a voice called across the lawn. 'If you're going out in the car, tell them to let me come! They won't let me, and it's not fair!'

I had prayed I wouldn't really find Davina. She deserved so much more than a quick goodbye, and there was no time for more. I spoke in urgent haste to a blur of sandy hair.

'I'm not going in the car. This is a secret but I'll tell you, I'm going away on my own. I'm leaving now.'

'I know where you're going,' she said triumphantly. 'To that nursing home place! Then I'll go with you, like you promised.'

I hissed at her in panic.

'Quiet! No, not there. At least, I don't think so.'

It was strange that at this moment realisation came to me that wherever I went, it could not be to the police with my fears and accusations. Despite Ralph's trickery, I could not betray him. Whatever he had done or planned to do, pity for him still lingered in my heart. He was a gentle, weak man in thrall to stronger and crueller wills.

Davina was insisting in a whisper,

'That nice doctor said . . . '

'I know what he said, but things are different now. Davina, I can't take you with me. I don't even know where I'll sleep tonight.'

'I don't care about sleeping! You'll need me to help you, anyway. We can pretend you're my mummy . . . '

I stood still, torn apart by her love and loyalty, and the obvious wrong of taking her with me into the unknown. But she made up my mind for me, grabbing my hand.

'Come on, let's go before someone sees us, or we'll never get away.'

I couldn't resist her. Right or wrong, I let her rush me down the drive and into the lane, a blur of gardens passing me by. Already, with the added confidence of Davina's company and help, a plan was forming. In St Dawes we could hire a car to take us out of this district, anywhere, just to find a hotel room and a respite to think.

All in good time, when I had safely escaped. But as yet, nothing was safe. It would be foolish to make for the village by the main road. When we were missed we would be followed, and that was the obvious route. But if we turned instead towards the sea, hid for a while, and then took the long way all along the cliffs, surely by the time we reached the village our pursuers would have combed the place vainly and turned elsewhere.

'Good idea!' Davina approved my muddled explanation. Then she was off again at top speed. 'Come on, I know where to hide. I'll show you!'

Around me, a world of shadows and shapes was all I saw of light and colour. But I knew we were out on the cliffs, as there was rough grass under my feet.

'They're coming!' Davina cried out suddenly.

'Who? Who's coming?'

'Someone's running after us!' She was peering back at the narrow track leading to the distant house. 'There's some cars, I can't quite see.'

I knew that despite all my struggles

for speed we had not really covered much ground. A few minutes more, just time enough to hide, might have saved us. But I decided, panting for breath, that if I must be taken back, I would need to be dragged back! Inch by inch they would have to drag me!

But for poor Davina it was different, and she was already in tears of disappointment and sheer fright.

'Go back, Davina!' I said quickly. 'Run home, say you're sorry. Say it was my fault, I made you go with me!'

'But I can't leave you here! Not here on the cliffs!'

'Yes, you can. Listen, sometimes I can see just a little.'

'Can you really see?' Her voice was full of wonder.

One moment more she hesitated. But then a distant sound, a man's voice shouting, made her jump with fear. I had no need to tell her again to run safely home.

'Auntie, you know the steps are just along here, and they go down to that

163

little hut place where people go in to watch the birds? You hide in there, and later on I'll come back and find you.'

I squeezed the small clinging hand before it broke away.

I stumbled on a few more yards. I must be near, very near, to the edge of the cliffs, for the turmoil of water below filled my ears. But I found no steps, no hiding place. My feet were sliding away from me in the damp grass.

Just one last thing I understood, a pounding of footsteps, a voice calling my name. I called back, in desperate fear, in hopeless longing.

'Harvey, I'm here!' But the cry was lost in the rush of the tide, in the swooping screams of sea birds.

Without mercy, rocks and earth tore away from my hands. Then there was nothing. I fell, and all the world fell with me.

6

I realised slowly that I was still alive. Living, breathing, feeling, and most of the feeling was pain.

I must have slithered down a long way. When I dared to look up, the top of the cliff seemed far above, against a fair and innocent blue sky dappled with breezy white cloud. Only this rough, shelf-like projection from the cliff-face had stopped my fall headlong to the scattered boulders and frothing tide beneath. Even now, one instant of dizziness could send me hurtling down.

At this moment I could see every detail of my grave peril, the ghastly drop beneath, the blood on my clinging hands. How long could I keep holding on for my life with these bruised and weakened fingers?

I tried to cry out, but my voice was carried away on the stiff sea-breeze. But there were other sounds, stumbling, scraping sounds, a gasping of painful breath.

In my desperation I had cried out Harvey's name. It wasn't Harvey who was so slowly, so painfully attempting the perilous descent to reach me.

'Ralph,' I wailed. 'Go back! You can't hold on with one hand!'

If he heard, he made no sign. For a moment I could not watch because he very nearly fell. Again came that gasp of pain. It took an eternity for him to inch down the wall of rock, all the time struggling, sliding, slipping. The last few feet were almost too much. Indeed, it was more luck than all else that brought him to my side.

'I've made it,' his soft familiar voice panted. And then, 'Oh, God!'

As an arm encircled me, for an instant I shrank from it, my relief at his safety turning to fear. Would it not suit his plans perfectly, his and his family's, to have me plunge to my death?

Had he really risked his own life to

help me or to ensure I didn't survive?

It was a question I never asked. As I looked full into his face for the first time, straight into his eyes, I saw the depth of his concern for me. He wasn't here to destroy me. No man who looked at a woman as Ralph looked at me could bring about her death.

'Don't move, stay very, very still, Lucy. I'll help you hold on.' He still could hardly manage to speak. 'I sent Davina for help, back to the house. The police will know what to do. They were arriving when I ran after you . . .'

I didn't really understand. I knew only that I could trust this man whose arm was sustaining me. And he kept on finding reassuring words.

'We'll be all right but we mustn't move till they come. This ledge isn't wide, and it's quite a dangerous drop to the beach.'

'It's straight on to the rocks and the sea!' I whispered. 'I can see it all!'

'You can see it?'

This wasn't the time or place for

shocks, but I was beyond considering that. I watched him peering at me eagerly, and there was belief dawning in his eyes. They were blue, gentle eyes in a young, fair face grey with fear and pain.

And then he smiled at me, and said simply, 'Hello!' I had never imagined that appealing smile.

'Oh, thank God, Lucy! I've read about such things. I suppose the shock and the fall. But did you understand what I said just now? That the police are at the house? I'm sure you'll guess why, after all you said last night. Some of Matt's plans must have backfired badly.'

'Please,' I whispered, 'don't tell me. Don't worry about it yet.'

'No, I have to tell you! It has to be now, in case . . . ' The soft voice wavered. 'When we're safe and sound on top, I'll tell them the whole story, I'll confess everything. But let me tell you first. I've wanted to so many times. Lucy, you've never known where Matt

168

works, have you? It's in the office of your grandfather's solicitors.'

'Oh!' I breathed.

There were two quite separate memories springing to life. I remembered visiting that office for Senor while he was ill, and being attended to by a quiet, efficient clerk with chilly eyes behind gold-rimmed spectacles. I remembered too that some clerk calling at Senor's house while I was playing the piano: he explained some documents to us, and chatted very pleasantly about our country retreat.

'Matt has been juggling with correspondence and managing the phone calls. In his own way he's a clever man. And I was a party to all of it. But I have to tell you something far worse than that,' Ralph was stumbling on.

'Ralph, I don't want to know!' It hurt me to see his pain and shame.

There was desperation in his voice now. 'You see, at first it was just the money, but when I met you, when I got to know you, that didn't matter

169

anymore. I just wanted you to be happy . . . Oh, how can I say this? . . . '

At this instant I was the stronger. I said gently, 'You've always been kind to me. But, Ralph, if you needed money, you only had to ask! It's still yours now, as much as you want!'

'No!' he broke in wildly. 'You still don't know the worst part!'

'I think I do. I've worked it all out. I was meant to die, wasn't I? — '

I got no further than that. I didn't hear whatever he answered. There were other sounds coming from above, movements, voices, and one authoritative voice calling clearly, 'Are you all right, down there?'

'They've come!' I cried out, and foolishly jerked upwards to see what was happening. The sudden movement brought giddiness sweeping back.

'I won't let you fall.' Once more the gentle, expressive blue eyes looked into mine, in sorrow, in shame, with great tenderness. 'I wouldn't harm you for all the world. I love you,

Lucy. I love you very much.'

It was the last thing I really understood. I knew there were men's voices, and ropes and rescue equipment, and a quick and competent operation being started to bring us to safety. But exhaustion overwhelmed me.

At the top of the cliffs I was laid down on a blanket or a coat. But there could be no comfort or relief when I saw ominous dark uniforms.

'It wasn't his fault,' I kept trying to say. 'It wasn't his fault.'

I didn't know if anyone answered. Before losing consciousness I could hear only the wild voices of those soaring sea birds disturbed from their lofty roosts . . . and one scream so like a human cry of terror that I never wanted to hear them again.

★   ★   ★

The hospital world was muddled and unreal, but so very familiar. I had

171

known it all before, this slow awakening to kind, brisk voices, to unseen helping hands. Nurses and doctors said the things they always said. Other more alarming voices asked official questions which I couldn't begin to answer, though I did my best. I kept repeating, 'It wasn't his fault.' It was all vague and unreal.

Time was a blur, day and night rolled into a confused whole. When the impossible questions came again I was actually dressed and on my feet, feeling rested and stronger. One thing I was quite certain about. I wouldn't stay one day longer than need be in this hospital limbo when poor Davina might be needing me.

'No, my dear, you don't have to stay here.' Sister Shaw amazingly agreed with me. 'All the bumps and scrapes are doing nicely, Dr Morley is very pleased with you. And it's all arranged for you to go to your friend's house this morning. You'll be taken down to transport at eleven.'

It was hugely puzzling, because I had no friends here. I had a family, but they weren't my friends! Down in a lift, and then a chilly plastic chair, and another confusion of voices . . .

'Miss Gray is for Rosedene Cottage, Bliston Cove,' someone was instructing the driver.

I corrected, 'No, I'm Mrs Devereux! Shouldn't I be going to Cliff House?'

They assured me my destination was Rosedene Cottage. The only explanation I could think of was that Ralph had arranged this for me, probably to stay for a while with some local people he knew.

The air outside seemed cool and damp. Some sort of ambulance was waiting. Inside the vehicle I was strapped into a seat, and there was a rail to hold as it swayed through quiet lanes. A talkative man with a plastered leg told me in detail how he slipped down a step.

'Going home to your family, are you?' he asked me pleasantly.

'There's just my husband,' I started to say, and then I stopped short.

Indeed, I had been blind in every way not to realise why no-one would talk to me about Ralph. They were sparing me the truth until I was a little stronger. But I knew now what the truth must be, why he couldn't come to me. He would have been arrested, he would be facing very serious charges.

'Here we are. Rosedene Cottage,' the driver announced.

The air was even chillier than when I left the hospital, and I was shivering. The man guided me to a gate.

'No!' I resisted suddenly. 'My husband isn't here, is he? I can't stay, I have to go to him. Look, if you could just drop me off at a police station — '

'Don't you worry, dear, everything's been taken care of,' the man soothed. 'You'll be looked after here.'

I heard a door open, hurried footsteps approaching.

'It's all right, Lucy,' a quiet voice said.

It was then that all my strength faded completely. As the ambulance drove on its way I was being half-carried through a doorway, into the enclosing warmth of a room. There was a smell of new paint.

A child's eager voice called, 'Auntie! Auntie! It's me!'

'Now wait, Davina,' she was sharply hushed. 'You know your aunt isn't well! We'll make her comfortable here, Harvey, the sofa by the fire.'

I was laid on soft cushions, still clinging to the warm strength that had held me. The so-familiar voice asked, 'You know who I am, Lucy?'

I whispered, 'Yes, I know.' And then, with absurd formality considering how I was holding on to him, 'Thank you for letting me come here, Doctor Sheridan. I couldn't think where I was going and I didn't dare ask!'

'You know now where we are?'

'Yes, your aunt's and uncle's cottage.' I struggled to sit up. 'But, Mr and Mrs Stanford won't want me staying here.

175

They said they'd do anything to keep us apart! But I won't be a bother for long. Ralph will need me, and I shall stand by him. Whatever happens, I shall.'

'Lucy, I wanted to talk to you about Ralph. I arranged things so I could break it to you myself.

I said quite sharply, 'You needn't break anything to me. I know the police were waiting for him, and he was going to make a full confession. If he ends up in prison, well, I'll just wait for him.' I trailed off there.

'That's very like you. You have great loyalty. But you still don't understand all Ralph had to confess.'

'It doesn't matter,' I said wearily. 'If he and Matt have already robbed me right and left, it doesn't matter.'

'There's something else. Something that will matter to you far more than money.' Harvey took a long deep breath. His voice was still very quiet. 'Listen to me. You were never married to him. You were never his wife.'

My own voice sounded like a

stranger's. 'But he proved I was. You asked for the proof yourself.'

'The marriage certificate was a forgery. The wedding photo was also a fake. Nurse Greig impersonated you, aided by a wig. Matt works in the office of your grandfather's solicitors, and he noticed the grey outfit you wore when you called in there. Rita bought something similar for the photo.'

I could say nothing. Harvey's voice sounded a long way off.

'The first day Ralph came to see us at Hillside, and I rang the solicitor's to confirm his story, obviously it was Matt I spoke to. He's been handling all the business side of things very efficiently. And it was Ralph's job to manage the human angle, persuade you into a second marriage, really the first, of course. In a short while you genuinely would have been Mrs Devereux, and they'd have the Alvarez legacy safely in the family, their aim from the start.'

'How can he tell me all those lies?' I whispered. 'How could he?'

'Possibly his relatives used the California clinic as a bait. I don't know. Obviously they instructed him exactly what to say to you, but I do know he wouldn't have harmed you in any way. Especially after he fell in love with you. That was a big complication, because he was already engaged to Rita Greig.'

I gasped with shock. 'So that's why she hated me!'

'Yes. Of course, the family never really advertised for a nurse. She was involved from the start. She was cold-hearted enough to look on while her fiancé married you, or shall we say, married your grandfather's money. But she wasn't prepared to watch him fall in love with you. The big house was just rented for a few months, to give the appearance of a prosperous family — and to keep you safely isolated, of course.'

I just nodded. It all made sense.

Harvey was going on, 'Rita and the Wilsons had convinced Ralph that you hadn't long to live after your injuries in the motor accident. Not true, I assure you! So he thought in a few months he'd lose a temporary wife, gain a fortune and be free for Rita. But actually he started having ideas of his own. He intended doing all he could after the wedding to make you well, take you to specialists, never give up hope that you'd recover.'

'I can understand that.' In a strange calm now, my thoughts were cold and clear. 'I never, ever believed he was a willing party to murder.'

'We don't know what was planned,' Harvey said gently. 'It might have satisfied Matt to have you pay off his debts and foot all the future bills. But the motive was certainly there. That's why I called in the police, to prevent you being dragooned to the altar under false pretences.'

'So it was you who called them?' I wasn't even surprised about that.

'Yes. Ever since that weekend I stayed at the house I'd been trying to trace the marriage at the Registry, trying to speak to a different person at the law offices instead of Mr Gudge's assistant whom I always seemed to get. And finally I called there myself, and I saw Matt Wilson behind a desk. He didn't see me, but I certainly recognised him. I travelled straight down to Cornwall and went to the police with the whole story.'

I nodded, mumbling my thoughts aloud. 'I'll see that Ralph has the best defence there is, the very best, then maybe he'll get a lighter sentence.'

I squeezed Harvey's hand tightly. 'You've been so good to me, I'll never forget all you've done.' Deliberately then I let go of him. 'I said I'd stand by Ralph, and I'll still do that. Whatever else he did, he risked his life for me. And — he'll need help from someone, won't he?'

I heard my heart beating. I heard Harvey speaking, very softly.

'I knew you had great loyalty and compassion, but Ralph won't need either from you, Lucy. Not any more.' Was it just a delusion that I seemed to hear in this quiet room the wash and hiss of a hungering tide below a cruel cliff face? And the cry of a Sea bird that was so very like a wild human scream of terror?

'I watched when they rescued you,' Harvey said. 'But when Ralph's turn came, he fell. They lowered me down to where he landed.' The steady voice was shaking now. 'But he didn't need a doctor, just a friend. He knew me, and spoke to me. He tried very hard to tell me everything, all I've just been saying to you. The last thing he said was a message for you. Would I ask you please to forgive him? Or to try to forgive him?'

Hurt gripped me more deeply as I thought that Ralph ever doubted I would forgive him.

'I wish — I wish I'd been kinder to him,' I whispered. 'Now it's too late.'

'Lucy, he wouldn't want you to reproach yourself,' Harvey said gently. 'He had a very deep love for you, and was very happy to have saved your life.

He risked his for yours willingly and I believe he gave it gladly.'

It was then that all my pain dissolved suddenly into tears.

★ ★ ★

I had never been a wife. I was not a widow. But my shock and sorrow were very deep. Though I sat at this friendly fireside surrounded by such care and sympathy, it seemed as if no warmth could reach me.

I heard the Stanfords expressing their regret about our last meeting, explaining that their attitude had appeared right to them at the time, insisting that I was indeed welcome now under their roof. I heard them as well trying to quieten an excited Davina who was running around in everyone's way.

Her family was away, she confided at last, she wasn't sure where or for how long. It didn't seem to worry her unduly, though she sobbed a little for 'poor Uncle Ralphie.'

Mrs Stanford bustled her off to the kitchen to help with the lunch. 'Lucy, you sit here and talk to Harvey. Just make yourself at home,' she invited me.

For the present, among these kindly people, I wasn't alone. But they weren't my own people, they had their separate paths to follow, and Harvey Sheridan, my dream for so long, had his own full, busy life.

'I suppose you'll go back to Hillside View?' I asked him.

'As soon as I can. I left a locum looking after things.'

'Well, will you take the message for me to Miss Aylmer? I never did get her real letter. The one Molly read out started off all wrong instead of 'Lucy dear,' and it had never been near a bottle of lavender water in its life. Miss Aylmer radiates lavender like Rita radiates spearmint.'

Huddled on the end of the sofa, I could hear him moving about the room. I was glad he was keeping his distance.

'What will happen now to Davina?' I asked.

'It's not certain. She could be placed in a suitable foster home.'

'No! Couldn't I take her?'

'You?' I imagined the deeply questioning look he must be giving me.

'I'll find a nice, friendly boarding school in the country, and meantime I'll go to that rehabilitation place you recommended.' I plunged on, 'And I want to adopt her legally. If it means fighting court cases, I'll fight them! What do you think?

'Can I suggest some amendments? First, I'm not sure about the rehab centre just yet. Ralph told me your sight had come back a little. I always felt there was hope and now I'm sure of it. I'll arrange some tests for you as soon as possible. Here's the second amendment, I'm not sure it would be possible for you to adopt Davina. Quite apart from your sight, you're a young girl completely alone. But there might be a way around it. If you found yourself a husband to share the responsibility — '

'A husband?' I said wearily.' Someone prepared to take on a wife who may or may not see, plus someone else's little girl in exchange for a joint bank account? No, I don't think so!'

'No? Would you still distrust an offer of marriage if it came from me?'

'From *you*?' I felt as if the skies fell, the world stopped revolving.

'And sign over all those financial assets of yours to your favourite charities tomorrow if you've a mind to. It's just you I want, not a penny of your money,' he chided me gently. 'I've tried hard to hide my feelings for Mrs Devereux, but I thought I'd made a poor job of it. I tried hard as well to believe I felt sorry for you, no more than that. But when you left Hillside, the truth hit me. I missed you. I missed you every day, every hour.'

I felt his hand close on mine.

'But there's one thing I must tell you. You're not the first girl I've loved. There was Gabrielle, and I swore, after

185

Gabrielle, that I'd never marry. You might have heard some sordid versions, but this is the truth. I saw her dance only once. The next day she was knocked down in the street near the theatre. I did what I could for her, but her legs were so badly injured . . . I took her off to France to recuperate. Nothing else mattered but getting her well.'

'You must have loved her very much,' I said softly.

'It didn't do either of us much good. When we arrived in a Paris hotel, someone recognised her, and told her that her husband was dying. He was some years older, a wealthy business-man. That was the first I knew of any husband. I took her straight to the house, where we found him making out a fresh will to cut her out completely. Well, that did something very strange to Gabrielle . . . '

I had to wait a moment while he steadied his voice.

'Yes, she told him I'd seduced her,

kept her away from him by force, she'd really loved him all the time and always would. Her husband immediately summoned up a henchman to throw me out. Like a fool, I didn't go quietly. It took the local gendarmerie to separate us and count the damage.'

I said weakly, 'That sounds awful!'

'Doesn't it just? Can you imagine the newspaper headlines? **The Doctor and the Dancer**. Not very good publicity for an honoured profession. When it was all over, I banished myself to India to work. I was there quite a while.'

'And Gabrielle?'

'Her husband did die, she became a wealthy woman, and promptly married a handsome young artist. I don't know where she is now. Lucy, I didn't mean to tell you all this at present — nor to mention marriage so soon. But perhaps you'll think about it?'

'I've thought!' I said simply. 'And the answer is yes . . . because I love you so much.'

These few moments had taught me

much about Harvey, a man not devoid of faults, no stranger to trouble and even disgrace. Yet he had come through unembittered, with a patient, penetrating, healing insight into human nature. As he took me in his arms, his lips on mine were warm, infinitely tender. And then I felt at last I had truly come home.

I sat quietly beside him, with my head resting against his shoulder, while the Stanfords came in and Davina pranced around, and everyone seemed pleased for us.

It was a little later that I let my hand stray gently, questingly over his face as I murmured. 'I just wish I knew . . . if you look how I've always imagined you.'

He drew back in mock alarm.

'Please, don't let anyone disillusion you just yet! But one day, please God, you'll see for yourself.' His voice suddenly was deeply grave, 'I promise, my darling. I promise.'

I held his dear hand against my face.

Whatever I might see in the future, my own imagined Harvey would live on unchallenged in my heart, a man ever young in resolution, a man ever handsome in integrity. A man to love always, always as I loved him now.

THE END

We do hope that you have enjoyed reading this large print book.

Did you know that all of our titles are available for purchase?

We publish a wide range of high quality large print books including:
Romances, Mysteries, Classics
General Fiction
Non Fiction and Westerns

Special interest titles available in large print are:
The Little Oxford Dictionary
Music Book, Song Book
Hymn Book, Service Book

Also available from us courtesy of Oxford University Press:
Young Readers' Dictionary
(large print edition)
Young Readers' Thesaurus
(large print edition)

For further information or a free brochure, please contact us at:
Ulverscroft Large Print Books Ltd.,
The Green, Bradgate Road, Anstey,
Leicester, LE7 7FU, England.
Tel: (00 44) 0116 236 4325
Fax: (00 44) 0116 234 0205

BELLE OF THE BALL

Anne Holman

When merchandise is stolen from the shop where Isabel Hindley works, she and the other shop assistants are under suspicion. So when Lady Yettington is observed going out of the shop without paying for goods, Isabel accuses her lady-ship of theft, making her nephew, Charles Yettington, furious. But things are more complicated when Lady Yettington is put under surveillance, and more merchandise goes missing. Isabel and Charles plan to find out who is responsible.

THE KINDLY LIGHT

Valerie Holmes

Annie Darton's life was happiness itself, living with her father, the lighthouse keeper of Gannet Rock, until an accident changed their lives forever. Forced to move, Annie's path crosses with the attractive stranger, Zachariah Rudd. Shrouded in mystery, undoubtedly hiding something, he becomes steadily more involved in Annie's life, especially when the new lighthouse keeper is murdered. Annie finds herself drawn into the mysteries around her. Only by resolving the past can she look to the future, whatever the cost!

LOVE AND WAR

Joyce Johnson

Alison Dowland is about to marry her childhood sweetheart, Joe, when his regiment is recalled to battle, and American soldiers descend on the tiny Cornish harbour of Porthallack to prepare for the D-day landings. Excitement is high as the villagers prepare to welcome their allies, but to her dismay, Alison falls in love with American Chuck Bartlett. Amidst an agonising personal decision, she is also caught up in espionage, endangering herself and her sister.

OPPOSITES ATTRACT

Chrissie Loveday

Jeb Marlow was not happy to trust his life to the young pilot who was to fly him through a New Zealand mountain range in poor weather. What was more, the pilot was a girl. Though they were attracted, Jacquetta soon realised they lived in different worlds; he had a champagne lifestyle, dashing around the world, and she helped run an isolated fruit farm in New Zealand. Could they ever have any sort of relationship or would their differences always come between them?